LEGIONS OF GOD

LEGIONS OF GOD

A Distant Power Faces Humanity's Darkest Karma

NOEL WILHELM MCDOUGALL

Kravitz & Sons

INNOVATORS IN PUBLISHING, MARKETING AND ADVERTISING

Kravitz and Sons LLC
204 E Arlington Blvd. Suite B
Greenville, NC 27858

Published by Kravitz and Sons LLC.

ISBN: 979-8-89639-721-2 (sc)
ISBN: 979-8-89639-720-5 (e)

*Hostility
is as the fangs of a serpent,
its venom
potent enough to extinguish
the glory in all of mankind.
The only thing humanity's been
left with is faith.*

Table Of Contents

PROLOGUE

How many a times have we reflected on a wrongful action that we had done in our past and felt that which we call guilt? What if all the dark actions done by humanity don't necessarily come around as it is said but instead stay around?

Presently on our planet, there is an imbalance between right and wrong since the noble actions of our people are being overshadowed by those of the wicked for generations.

Many of us believe that when something of a wicked nature is committed, a divine punishment is sure to follow. This is not entirely true, for the Creator never hurts or destroys what he created. A self-destruction is more like it.

Could it be that all the evil activities in the world leave a stain behind, which later come back to haunt us? If so, then this is what we would say: Is a punishment from on high?

Many luminaries are sent to us from time to time, but we have killed them all and paid them very little interest. If these unworthy activities of ruthless people leave an evil karma, it could very well be stored somewhere in the far reaches of our galaxy, releasing tremendous negative energy unto the planet every number of years.

In this story, you will know what happens when dark actions are committed through centuries and what it takes to make them vanish.

ACKNOWLEDGMENTS

Special thanks to God and the Lord of Host for their enlightenment to the world.

For my wife, Maria Campos, who was very helpful and patient throughout the process of publication.

For Nathalie McDougall-my adorable only daughter. For Sarita McDougall-my mom who was supportive in the process of publication.

For my dad and the rest of my entire family.

CHAPTER 1

Lorraine is a moderate town in France, existing to this date. The inhabitants of this part of the country were rather strange, as the year was 1806.

Famine struck the town killing thousands of people. Relief was denied by its own government due to infectious diseases caused by corpses scattered across the land. Fields of crops, fruits, and thick vegetation were reduced to dust lands. Rivers and lakes ran dry. Nothing would survive. France did not have total protection against such disease that if within a five-hundred-mile radius, the filth in the air would enter your eyes, ears, and pores, eating the body's internal organs, causing blood to exit orally.

The remaining inhabitants were quarantined for eleven years. No one ever bonded with these survivors. They were called the "Forgotten 44." Four thousand four hundred people were still alive. Being isolated from civilization disabled their mental progress. Their hygienic standards remained neutral, being deprived from the outer society. Evolution had advanced. Sense of reason was no longer a part of their existence.

Some neighboring townspeople spoke of a curse that had been sealed on this town for hundreds of years by a shape-shifting angel of darkness because of witches burnt at the stake years earlier.

A large cloud of darkness had fallen over the land of Lorraine shortly after the famine had set in, depriving the Forgotten 44 sunlight.

It was said that this shape-shifter had been at war with God's undefeatable army for thousands of years. Being defeated on all terms, he gathered women and gave them supernatural abilities to implant evil in the hearts of people. The women were put to death at the infamous "burning at the stake" by the town of Lorraine.

A so-called curse remained on that town. Nothing grew any longer on condemned soil. No one entered, and no one left because the town was constantly on surveillance mode by army men.

In this town of Lorraine lived a unique, distinguished, but eerie family. A woman known to the locals only as Leena lived on the far outskirts of Lorraine. Being seen only at night and early dawn, with a shawl and hood over her head, her face had never been seen at a close range. Two other individuals believed to be of some relation to her also inhabited a castle-type home they owned on the far opposite end of Lorraine. A female and a male, though the male had never been seen in Lorraine, were believed to be her children-Clare and Indrid Cole. This trio was never affected by any of the tragedies that happened in their town. They seemed to be immune to all known and unknown sources. Their origin and identity were unknown, and their routine was unlike others. Their father was a sinister leader of a group of mutants, hell-bent on the destruction of human civilization so his breed of followers would run the planet. These mutants were able to control the function of the human brain. As for Leena, no one knew her past existence, but angels from heaven seemed to trace her whereabouts. Perhaps something lay within her, with great power. Even the occupants of Lorraine were fearful of her, though they were mentally disturbed.

Word reached the ears of the government in the French capital. With fear brewing on the horizon on what or who these people were, government officials suspected that these people had something to do with what was going on in this town. Some townsfolk believed Leena and her children were related to this shape-shifter that had sealed this land with damnation. This dark angel was said to have been seen at the base of a mountain entering a dark cave, its feet never touching the ground.

The army's general composed an assault on Leena and children to eliminate this threat.

For all this rime, Leena never did hurt a soul in all her existence, but she was about to encounter death against a group of French soldiers, armed with rifles. Late one evening as she stood near the window of her castle, she stared at the set of soldiers nearing her property. Though she had seen their thoughts even before their mission started, she remained calm. These people had not the least idea that they were about to commit a huge error. Leena would be a factor in their deliverance from this suffering.

These gunmen did not know what they were up against, with very little known about Leena. They decided to hold and see if they could take a good look at her. Their orders were to kill her.

Clare, her daughter, was not with her on that gloomy evening. No one knew her whereabouts or that of Indrid Cole's. He had never been seen in or around Lorraine.

Soldiers stood looking toward the entrance of Leena's home to wait for her sighting. About two hours later, a bright flash of light was seen by the soldiers inside the mansion. Slowly, the door opened; there stood this gorgeous, fearless, yet peaceful woman with a snowy white glow surrounding her stature. The hood she wore on the head was no more. That was the only noticeable detail of her at that moment, for the glow around her blinded her attackers.

Orders were given to fire at her. More than a dozen bullets hit her. As she fell to her knees, a faint, echoing voice was heard all around saying, "My dear son, my only crime was to be different from everyone on earth. Though my life was taken, my spirit shall exist where flesh and bones reside not. You will find me near from time to time. Carry on, for your days of invincible might awaits you. Look for your sister Clare. She is in great danger ." Leena died on her doorstep a short while after.

The soldiers were confuse at the voice of Leena, which they heard before she died. They were mumbling to one another about what they witnessed.

Indrid Cole heard his beloved mother's voice from a far-off land. Indrid Cole was described as an eerie tall individual wearing a long black trench coat with deep-black eyeballs. He was spotted in remote regions of London, England, one day before his mother was killed. Apparently, he used a telepathic form of communication only with his mom and sister Clare. Indrid always loved heights. On few occasions, he had been seen on mountains summits and high-rise buildings in and around London City.

Clare was similar to him in character, though a little more social with her fellow humans. The few friends she had were a bit spooked of her because of her origin.

CHAPTER 2

For more than twenty years, Indrid Cole was never seen in France. He was still a child when he was stolen from his home by his father's mutants. As time passed, he vanished from his father's sight.

He knew the time to return to Lorraine was at hand. He became airborne as he had the ability to do so because of his mother's gift of superhumans abilities, which was passed down to her apparently by angels from the Creator. It was a complex and binding ordeal for him and Clare because of a negative energy from their father. However, they had more good than evil in them.

Clare saw when her mother was murdered in a vision. She had sorrow in her beautiful blue eyes but remembered she still had one brother left and called for him. Indrid Cole heard her just before leaving for France.

The place was Ireland, and while she made her way to the top of an old lighthouse immediately, a group of violent and diabolical creatures were about to rip her to shreds but just in time a loud ringing sound was heard from above. A strong cold wind blew toward them. It waws Indrid Cole coming for his little only sister. The earth beneath them shook because of such force coming together.

The three creatures made a stand to proceed in battle against Indrid Cole, as Clare stood there watching in freight. Ingrid started walking toward the creatures with no emotion. As he walked, fire began to make its way ahead of him, engulfing the creatures and throwing them off a nearby cliff. What an awesome display of power it was for little sister Clare. Indrid later explained the attackers were ancient keepers of the bay.

"Good to see you after so long, big brother," spoke Clare. Indrid placed his hands on her cheeks and said, "The influence of Von Seth will be stopped."

It seemed like he spoke of that shape-shifter in Lorraine, France that remained in a cave.

Clare was seventeen years of age but insisted to support her brother on whatever strategy he would proceed.

It was obvious by now that Indrid Cole would cast a main role on the situation in Lorraine. A confrontation between him and Von Seth was near, despite the eruption of the famine that began a few years ago.

During this time, the body of Leena remained at the entrance of her home where she was shot to death. Perfectly preserved, with bullets lying around her, it seemed that just a small number of them had hit their target. Sure, Leena could have remained very much alive without a scratch, but this was her time for departure, for she was called on.

During the time Indrid Cole remained in Ireland with his sister, another menace started taking place. According to authorities, people of a rich settlement were being dragged out into the wood, slaughtered, and piled up one on top of the other in the center of a large pentagram sculpted on the ground. No one had seen or heard the culprit, for it struck at dusk or late night. Activities had led people to believe that there was more than one person or monster responsible for these heinous crimes. Reports showed that more than two civilians disappeared in one night at the same time every time the sun would set. Civilians were helpless against this culprit.

Word was out that a strange young man with a woman had been seen on the rooftop of building near the city. Some countrymen cried, "It is the devil and his wife that have come to take our riches."

Indrid Cole already knew their thoughts and who was stealing these people and murdering them in the bushes as well. He went into the presence of these wealthy citizens and said, "I shall end your fear and desperation and annihilate your offender if you believe me not to be the evil one. My name is Indrid Cole, and I am just as I am."

An old man in the crowd whispered to another beside him, "He has no eyes. I wonder how he sees."

Indrid Cole answered, "We are not from this world. We desire not your wealth or your food. We were sent here as bounty hunters to rid your planet of all evil." These words fell like a bomb to the people present, and they all paid their respect to Indrid and his sister.

Stepping back a few feet, he held his sister's hand, slightly knelt on one foot, and vanished in thin air. No one knew where they had gone.

Moments later, Indrid Cole stood facing the woods, awaiting the assault on this settlement. Moments after, a chanting arose from inside the sticks, making its way toward Indrid Cole. These things appeared to be hooded knights. Indrid stood his ground, for the field was open for a showdown between good and bad, outnumbering twenty to one.

Clare entered the confrontation and stood next to her brother, armed to the teeth with a variety of lethal weapons. The druids from hell stopped their march, for the way was blocked by an invincible opponent. It was late evening as the sun had set in Ireland as they stood face-to-face. The procession started again toward Indrid and Clare.

As the knights drew close, Indrid opened his shawl and lifted his forehead slightly. The druids drew swords and attacked.

Clare was still able to fight. She shot a brilliant razor-sharp disk and severed the heads of half-dozen attackers. Another swing of a sword grazed her leg. She stumbled on to the ground.

Indrid dispensed what appeared to be razor spears at his offenders-the velocity when launched was so strong that the bodies of the enemies were pinned to trees.

Four druids remained but did not dare to make a move on Indrid Cole. The ground opened because the mission was a failure, and they were swallowed at once.

All spears were sort of attached to Indrid's mechanical battle gear beneath his coat but became unseen when not in fight mode.

He moved toward Clare, took a look at his sister's injury, and placed the index finger over it. A strange substance appeared out of nowhere on the cuts on his sister. Less than a minute after, not even a scar remained on her. As Clare stood up, Indrid said to her that the enemies were sent by Von Seth. They were called the mercenaries from hell. He warned Clare that there might be more of them.

Many of the countrymen were eyewitnesses to this gruesome fight. As Indrid and his warrior sister made their way to the town square of this settlement, a little boy of around nine years of age walked out of the crowd of people present and said to Indrid and Clare, "When I grow up, I want to become just like you so my papa doesn't hurt me anymore. Thank you for taking my fear away."

Indrid stared at this young boy for a minute and drifted away as if with no interest. Everyone had dispersed and gone indoors, for it was becoming late night. The boy sat down in the corner of the street just outside the faint reach of the streetlamp lit up by town member volunteers and looked a these warriors moved away from him. As the youngster turned the opposite way, there stood Indrid and Clare right in front of him. He fell on his buttocks as he faced Indrid, looking up seven feet above him. Indrid Cole took out a strange polished metal object from a side pocket of his customized boot and told the little boy to wear it on his wrist at all times. It was a motion magnetic shield that would protect against violent physical abuse and could only be removed by the boy himself.

CHAPTER 3

Indrid and Clare took off and left Ireland at once. During this time, the Forgotten 44 were becoming more like animals, unable to know right from wrong, as they were being guarded by officials outside safe barriers.

Leena's body could not be removed because of fear of contamination. Though her body was different from human corpse, no one knew this. As she lay on the floor, it seemed as if she wasn't really dead because of this bright glow around her. It was quite a confusing situation for everyone in and around her hometown of Lorraine. Leena resided on the division of Lorraine and another town; therefore, the army could keep a close watch on any development where she lay dead.

Suddenly, an eerie feeling came across the entire country of France. The temperature started falling to near-freezing point. The winds began to strengthen. The soldiers guarding the mansion of Leena became very numb. They were unable to utter a word, as air pressure got to extreme levels. Blood was secreting down the ears of army officials that were near the home of Leena. The people in Lorraine somewhat ignored this phenomena happening, for they were as animals at this point. However, they were feeling the impact of this moment but were not affected as others.

Von Seth from deep inside his dark domain spoke in a rough double-chord voice, "Welcome to hell, Indrid Cole." Dark clouds from above were opened. A tremendous flash of lightning struck the ground in Lorraine. Indrid Cole and his sister stood before thousands of odd-looking people. Citizens all over France were struck in amazement. The heavens opened. Flashes of light were visible across the sky over a large area. Many sick, demented people moved slowly and cautiously toward Indrid and Clare and stopped just a few feet then would retreat with grunts and a little fear. Just under an hour later, they came into motion. Everyone was silent as the army awaited for a reason to intervene. Indrid and Clare remained motionless with no expression. Total blackness was in Indrids eyes. The wind blew through Clares long dark hair. It seemed as if they tilted their heads up to the heavens.

For the first time in many years, the sun shone through the breakage of dark clouds. People looked up above embracing the sunlight, forgetting how it felt to have the sunlight on them.

For all this time, the French army did not know that Indrid Cole and his sister had nothing but the purest intention to redevelop this land of Lorraine and prevent damnation of the entire continent. The French ruler deployed half his arsenal in full force armed with tanks, cannons, and more than a thousand soldiers with live ammunitions to nearby locations. They discovered what Indrid and Clare were capable of doing, for they had known about the happenings in Ireland.

These two heavenly warriors seemed to be at war with the whole world. Even so, they could not be destructed, as everyone stared at them with confusion. Clare said in a strange language to all who were present, "Return to your domain. Our mission is not of your concern at this time. You are in clear and present danger."

Astonishingly, everyone did as they were told but continued looking on from their corroded homes. Have in mind that these Forgotten 44 had no understanding whatsoever when spoken to, but they had when Clare gave them the order.

She told them this, for they all knew the military could make a strike at any time. Their arrival at Lorraine had a most peculiar influence on the atmosphere as the dark clouds above faded, and the sun's rays started to enter.

For throughout this time, the Forgotten 44 were surviving only on decayed food left from a long time in the past and some spotty vegetation.

Indrid and Clare moved like the beam of a flashlight from the spot they were to the mansion of Leena. As they entered the gates making their way to their beloved mother, they both extended their arms. A ball of light surfaced on the palm of their hands, and they placed it over Leena. Suddenly, her body vanished. Not even a trace on where it went remained. Something so unbelievable took place shortly after. The home of Leena also had vanished from the face of the earth. Nothing but the piece of land where I once stood was left. It was as if Leena and the home she occupied was just a reflection in a mirror. Only Indrid and his sister knew what took place.

The army base was near five hundred miles away, but some soldiers were based a little closer looking on with long-range binoculars. They were speechless at what they saw. A message was sent at once to the general, for these military men feared what would be next since they had fired and killed Leena. But Indrid had something else in mind, Von Seth, the demonic creature that roamed nearby.

The temperature had gone back to normal, and winds diminished but remained partially gloomy. Indrid said to Clare, "Von Seth shall not raise a battle against us. His strength does not equal two. I will find him when the time is right."

CHAPTER 4

They both made their way to the presence of the entire French army. The base was guarded by some two hundred armed soldiers and a tall-gated fence. A long stretch of highway connected this main base with a major city twelve miles away named Alsace, although some people lived nearby on the roadside. It was broad day light as these two strange individuals made their way along this military highway when a woman of about twenty-two years of age came out from a cutoff road with a hefty stallion and said to Indrid, "Please don't harm me. I would just like to get across the highway to the grasslands so my horse can eat."

Indrid asked her to come closer, so the young woman took a few feet forward but in much fear then stopped. Indrid asked her, "Where is your home, earthling?"

The girl replied, "I live a half mile behind the military base."

Indrid then asked, And this fine beast you carry, does he reside with you? Or is he the chief commander of your defending force?"

The young woman answered, I do not understand, but I love animals, and they love me and have no evil in them."

Indrid said to her, If an animal is unable to reason and yet exists without eternal evil, then the entire human race shall remain in darkness until your great redeemer returns and deliver you from damnation."

The young woman was astonished at what she was told and asked, Where do you people come from?"

Clare, who was also present, spoke, "We exist on a parallel universe with yours a million light-years away.

The girl said to Indrid Cole, "You are a wise and handsome man, mister, but with a peaceful voice."

Indrid said in a serious but calm voice, "Your remarks are embraced but are like a bowl of sugar falling into a great ocean. The young damsel then moved on with her four-legged friend.

A short while after, Indrid and his companion were visible by the army base. Cannons and soldiers heavily armed looked on int the distance as the two extraterrestrials came closer. Indrid Cole and Clare moved straight forward with an arsenal from outside this world. At approximately one hundred yards away, Indrid Cole was confronted very cautiously by a cavalry on horseback that was sent by the general to investigate their presence.

Face-to-face with Indrid, just under two hundred horsemen raised their pistols and took aim at the two visitors. Few villagers looked on in suspense awaiting the gunshots, eager to see blood, for in this time and age, humans were ruthless and dominant.

The captain said in a loud voice, "Retreat or face death, for this land is ours."

Clare stared at Indrid, then at the captain on his horse. She slowly turned toward all the soldiers from one far end to the other, vigilant for any sudden move.

Indrid spoke, "If your marksmanship is perfect, even at close range your weapons would still be insignificant. Your success is based on power and greed."

The captain shouted in anger, "You stand here with nearly two hundred guns pointed at you, and still you insult me. I shall have my men tear you into shreds, you insolent bastard!" He gave an order to some of his comrades to teach him a lesson.

Indrid turned to the soldiers drawing their swords and froze them instantly, making them immobile. Sword's fell to the ground. Indrid then asked the captain, "Do you wish to proceed?"

The captain then said, "I shall kill you myself!" He got off his horse and rushed toward Indrid with his gun in hand. When in front of Indrid, he stood near six feet tall, when Indrid was much taller in stature. The captain aimed up to Indrid s forehead. The gun barrel could barely reach Indrid's brow. Indrid covered the mouth of the gun barrel with his index finger. A loud bang was heard, but the bullet was plastered at the tip of the pistol.

The frightened captain started shaking like a scared sick animal and begged for his life to be spared, saying in a pleading tone, "I only take orders from the chief commander. It is my duty. I have a family to feed, and I liked you folks from the very start."

Indrid told him, "Return to your headquarters and tell your commander to gather all rulers from this part of your world, for I have a message to them and their people. It happens in seven earth days."

The scared chief replied, "Yes, sir, I will deliver your request at once."

The cavalry rode away to their base. Indrid and his sister went down on one knee and were airborne with a thundering velocity. No one knew where they were vanished to.

The captain said to the chief commander, "Sir, we have a major situation. This man is not a man like us. He is something else much powerful than anyone I know. There is a woman, who also goes along with him. She stands behind him."

We shall do as he pleases, answered the chief commander. He immediately contacted all government organizations from around the continent and told everyone to make haste to France for an important meeting in an open stadium just outside Alsace.

Meanwhile, the Forgotten 44 began to communicate with one another by hand signal, for they had forgotten how to use their tongue. But for some hidden reason, the atmosphere remained almost the same in Lorraine, even after the arrival of Indrid Cole.

As for Von Seth, he was not seen by anyone for some number of years. It was almost as if he hibernated for a full year. Some folks in other villages even said that whoever saw this creature would die in eight days.

One day before the grand meeting, Indrid and his companion reappeared. They were seen on a back city street somewhere in Germany by none other than an estranged friend Clare had as a youth. The woman looked on as if trying to figure out this familiar face. Clare turned and recognized who this young woman was. They walked up to greet each other.

The girl said in suspense, "I cannot believe it is you I'm seeing."

Clare answered, "I knew we would in time meet again. Even though I did not enter your school, you were not alone in your training."

The young woman answered, "I have much to thank you for all you have taught me," at several moments taking a quick glance over at Indrid Cole standing some few feet away.

Clare took her longtime friend by the hand and told her, "Come with me. I have someone I would like you to meet."

Indrid stood next to a monument, facing the other way, as usual with no expression on his face, though it was difficult to even look at his face, because of fear, much less see an expression on him.

Clare said to Indrid, "Brother!" Indrid turned around facing them.

The friend, who was at a loss, muttered with a shaky, trembling voice, "My dear friend, I thought you were alone in this world, but now you have not just a friend but a brother and protector, charming and gentle looking."

Clare said to Indrid, "This young woman was and still is a great friend of mine whom I met before you found me. She dedicated most of her time to the study of evolution and science."

Indrid spoke gently, "I thank you, young edagenuine friendship to Clare and the will you have to succeed in your quest for knowledge of the unknown. It is greatly encouraged by myself and peers, and it also shall serve you well, yet sometimes knowledge of higher magnitude should be accompanied by another kind of wisdom. I am pleased to meet you, Tandoor. May you always be at peace"

Tandoor was a little confused and shocked at the words of Indrid and said, "How can this brother of yours know all this information? And on the other hand, he even knows my identity. Clare, where did he come from? He is magnificent!"

Clare said to her friend, "There is much for you to know, but in time." Clare held her longtime friend by the hand and told her, "Peace be with you. I shall see you again before I am gone."

Tandoor asked in concern, "Are you going to die soon? Are you ill?"

Clare said to her, "I will exist until he who created me is ready."

With that being said, Tandoor found herself standing alone,as she turned and turned with unease trying to understand what just happened.

CHAPTER 5

The day in which this individual known as Indrid Cole would deliver a great message to the people from this part of the world had come. It was already midday. The entire French army were standing by, well armed but willing to listen, along with other rulers from other countries. The conference was to be held in a large open ground a short distance from the military base. Somewhere around twenty thousand people were present from nearby towns and villages, eager to witness what would happen.

As the evening hours rolled on, a long line of smoke or dust was seen overhead. The winds started once again. Suddenly, Indrid Cole and his supporter known as Clare appeared in the center of everyone, with full-grey body suit extended to the head and with a white cape and a far more advanced weapon than anything the military could ever operate attached to their upper shoulder. Everyone was speechless and sort of uncomfortable at the presence of these beings. Indrid stood motionless with his arms in fold and with a straightforward look.

Clare began to speak in a moderate echoing voice similar to when Leena spoke just before she died, "Our presence on your land is to cause harm to no one but to exhort you, all, on this earth of perdition. My name is Urvenus. Your negative actions—such as greed, fallible judgment, and wars—attract evil on your people."

Then Indrid Cole unfolded his arms and spoke, "It is not our desire to govern your earth or to wage war against its citizens, but when your careless actions extend outside your world, they become our concern. The lack of rational intelligence on the will to establish peace in your world causes a negative energy that extends far beyond your reach. We exist on a parallel plane such as yours, several light-years from your galaxy.

"Over the centuries, we have established a higher method of connections and understanding with the Creator of all that is and is not. Our reward is an extremely higher technological manufacture equal with a devotional respect and conduct to our neighbors and our maker. I am Uriel, son of Celine, who was a foundation for our mission on this planet. Her agenda here was complete; therefore she was sent back through time to be regenerated. Our creation numbers in millions, with no need for warfare, for he who was sent to us ended it all, brought forth a new revolution for all existing worlds. However, our wish is not to terminate human life-forms but the evil backlash that is created. But if a dangerous threat is acknowledged, we will be forced to engage a defense mode, and destruction of retaliation is better not tested. Von Seth, a powerful angel of darkness, resides among you, all, and though you do not know it, no arsenal you possess can stop him, let alone kill him He makes the blackened heart his puppet and the noble his target. As for Indrid Cole, I am in him, and he is in me."

During this time, everyone was so silent that not even a breath was heard.

A government agent shouted, "How can we believe in your word? That it is not dominion over our nations that you seek and that you posses such magnificent attire and power?"

Urvenus replied, "If the beasts of the fields are of a lower nature than humans, their accomplishments are indeed of very little interest to you, all, and if their intelligence would be at the level of humans, they would crave what you posses."

A Roman leader asked, "What is your reward for such a very long, distant journey on a mission that should be of no use to both of you?"

Uriel spoke, Tt is of no concern to us how you run your world within its orbit, for that lies in you to replenish your violence and arrogance against another of your own kind. If you do not acknowledge and restore a peaceful and free world so that all territories are open to all men, then your suffering and afflictions shall plague you, all, until all greed, selfishness, and dominion over others be terminated, for so being that a man of your kind cannot govern something that he did not create. The institutions and functions of all worlds were constructed by the one who is the unseen from all mortal eyes; therefore, his instructions and institutions must be followed and upheld over man's authority and earthly law. As for a reward unto us, it is of no need."

A well-known and respected individual from in between the nation rulers asked these two strange and powerful beings, "What is the content of your knowledge on the situation in Lorraine?"

Urvenus replied, "It is a plague that has fallen on you, a residue of your corrupt earthly desires and evil actions. If you do not make haste to discover the right way to exist, it shall one day destroy the lives of many humans. This message has been transmitted to you people from three centuries into the future. If you, all, should be victorious in your quest for a peaceful world, then his kingdom will be established on your earth. He who returns unto you shall show you the way and will redeem this entire planet. Von Seth, who is a production of evil thoughts and the negative actions of you earthlings, took on a life force of his own. Now he is unstoppable by anything of this earth. We shall intend to erase him but not forever, for that depends on you, all."

CHAPTER 6

Just as this statement was over, Uriel quickly instructed everyone at the conference to disperse, for a great danger was detected. He could feel the shock waves caused by the nearness of Von Seth.

Apparently, Von Seth was determined to face his nemesis. It had been a number of years that he remained in that cave. Just on very few occasions was he spotted by humans near the mountain base. No one had seen this creature up close in the face, but local rumors were heard around the land that he glided through the air and carried a hatchet as his right arm.

Suddenly, Urvenus was grabbed and dragged forcefully by something invisible for a few feet from where she was standing. She turned her body into solid ice form, still allowing her to move even being frozen solid, due to being touched by this entity. Her freezing body disabled the stealth of whatever it was that had gotten hold of her, and for just a few seconds, a quick look at Von Seth was possible. Urvenus was free from his grasp, but right at that instant, Von Seth vanished before thousands of eyes.

Uriel said to Urvenus, "He remains among us. I can see him though he doesn't realize it. His existence is made up of rapid-moving microorganisms that appear like hot ashes unseen to the naked eye. His molecules decrease in velocity when the opposite of heat touches him; otherwise, he is able to control stealth mode at his will."

People were still near, for they did not know what was happening. Some ran for safety when they saw Urvenus being dragged violently, but most were rather peculiar to understand what was that thing they just saw for a number of seconds. Yet Uriel repeated to them all, "Move. Get to your home and stay clear." Uriel could see this unseen creature because of his extremely powerful thermal eyesight that could penetrate right through steel. That would explain the reason for the eerie and intimidating look of his eyes.

Urvenus was ready for retaliation. Although she could not see Von Seth, she had total help from her brother in keeping her informed.

Once again, Von Seth confronted his enemies. This time he went for Uriel. He was still unseen, making his assault from behind. When in just a few feet away from his rival, he strangely found himself unable to move even while being stealthy. Uriel had paralyzed his mobility, since he had the unique ability to control and manipulate everything that would move on the earth, including the weather. However, to keep Von Seth paralyzed was draining energy right out of him, for the fact that Von Seth was a beast with much power, fighting to be able to go free. On split seconds, he would become visible but would shift back to stealth during his struggle to break loose.

In complete amazement, everyone still present at this meeting could see Uriel and Urvenus, but they could not see who else was there. Uriel had a connection to the one who was believed to be his estranged father, who also possessed this power, though very little was known of this individual.

Von Seth moaned like an animal struggling to set free. When suddenly Uriel stood face-to-face with him for about half a minute, he then vanished once more.

The soldiers present were somewhat nervous on what they should do. The entire army along with their government looked on to figure out what was with these two strange beings.

In an instant, an explosion was heard and felt. Von Seth was totally free in flesh and bones. He broke the paralyzation on himself and was out in the open before many people. The army fired a cannon on the direction of the explosion, right at the spot where Uriel and Urvenus stood. The blast of the cannonball tore a large hole in the ground, causing chunks of dirt and debris to be blown into the air. Uriel and Urvenus stood in the very same place with the cannonball lying at their feet, with not even a scratch found on them.

As the smoke and dust cleared, what stood before these people was unimaginable. The fangs on this creature were fine razor-sharp, exposing cheekbones, with rags of clothing covering a portion of his odd-looking body. Despite all, he had the shape of a human, although very different. One of his arms appeared to have been ripped off around the upper elbow, perhaps in some ancient war, but he seemed to have attached a very dangerous weapon where it was severed. It was still daylight hours, and Von Seth had never been seen by the light of day, for his movements of activity would always take place at nightfall. People at the scene were terrified but still felt secure due to warriors being present.

The army's chief commander shouted, "Soldiers, stay put! Whatever this thing is, fire at my command!"

Von Seth grinded those horrible fangs together while staring at Uriel and Urvenus from several yards away but didn't dare to attack, at least not yet. His attention was then directed to the country leaders seated on a platform in front of armed soldiers.

Uriel knew that to exterminate this creature would be extremely fatal for all human lives that were present.

The monster moved forward to eliminate the groups of earthly government officials all at once. Around two hundred soldiers fired rounds of live ammunitions straight at Von Seth.

Smoke filled the air. Far off on the horizon, almost directly over Lorraine, there was brightness where it was darkness. All the gloom had disappeared, but just as it was gone, it returned.

As the smoke cleared, Von Seth was seen facedown on the ground but suddenly rose to an upright position as if an invisible coil lifted him. Since he wore a type of clothing that ran down to ground level, it was difficult to see if his feet were reaching the ground. There was no bullet damage on any part of his mutilated body. This beast remained intact as if nothing had hit him.

Everyone that was there ran for their lives. Some elder people collapsed, for what they had seen was too unbelievable to take easy.

The general ordered a cannon blast at Von Seth, but Uriel—in the strike of lightning—moved right in front of the general and ordered him to abort his command. The army general said to him in a hasty tone, "Have you not seen with your own eyes that this animal must be killed? He has been shot by two hundred men and still standing there as if waiting for more. A direct cannon blast he will not survive."

Uriel answered the general, "Don't you remember that I said to you no weapons you hold can ever destroy him? For he is not human, neither an animal from this world. His life force does not rely on a pulse or the need of internal organs. He carries none. Understand that he was brought forth to life by your actions. You cannot fight your own reflection, for wars of demons last for thousands of years."

Uriel then turned and made his way over to meet his fate. As he confronted his opponent, he extended his arms. His black eyeballs turned into like a bright glowing green light. The winds began to blow slightly, then a little faster. The temperature began to fluctuate from warm to cold. A powerful bolt of lightning struck the ground right next to Von Seth, causing a circle of frozen earth surrounding him.

This activity seemed a little too risky for Von Seth to attempt anything. He looked around in rage at people hiding nearby then turned to Uriel and Urvenus. Pointing at them with his hatchet arm, he began spinning his body at high speed releasing dust and suddenly vanished into nothing.

Uriel assured he was gone, but for a short time only. Urvenus tnen ssaaiiud. to the countries' head officials who were still there, "We shall meet with you, all, in time to come. For your safety, stay clear from in between."

Uriel and his assistant left, but as they drifted away, a young woman went into their presence and said, "Clare, it is me, Tandoor. We met a little over a week ago in Germany."

Clare remembered her friend and embraced her warmly.

Tandoor then turned to Uriel and said, "How do you do, mister? I am completely astonished for what I just saw. You both are wonderful individuals. I cant believe I'm standing in front of a spaceman and his sister. I love everything about your kind, much more from you, mister. Your knowledge is inaccessible by people from this planet!" Tandoor was so excited she couldn't stop shaking. She looked at Clare and said, "I'm starting to feel a special attraction to this brother of yours. If he were to ever accept me, I would put all my love in his hands, leave my every activity to be next to him. He is one like no other!"

Clare stared at her and smiled slightly, understanding why this girl felt this way about her massive brother.

Uriel knew what this young woman was thinking but couldn't make any sense out of it, so he said nothing on the remarks of Tandoor but kept staring at her for a while. Uriel knew nothing about physical and emotional attraction to that of a female from this earth, and so they walked on for several miles back to Alsace.

On the way, they were confronted by highway thieves, who demanded anything with value. Uriel and his female companions stopped and remained still as four notorious delinquents stood before them. Uriel knew these were humans, so he could no retaliate until a threat was presented. The thieves were armed with sticks and knives as they slowly walked toward this humanlike being and his associates.

When they were in front of Uriel and Urvenus, they held back, thinking if they should proceed with their crime due to the awesome sight of these individuals. These robbers were as children in comparison to Uriel. Glancing at a small portion of weaponry hidden beneath his shawl, they became slightly afraid. Even the eerie look of this seven footer couldn't quench the thirst for robbery in these men.

Urvenus did not move or made the slightest twitch, since she knew no one could harm them.

Tandoor then said to these men, "You, all, must leave at once. We are not seeking trouble with anyone!"

The thieves then replied, "If you are not looking for trouble, then trouble is looking for you. This is an assault, and you must give us what is asked from you, or you shall die!"

Tandoor knew what her friends were capable of, for she was present at the large conference that had ended a while ago and was an eyewitness to what took place between that destructive beast and the military and her now two friends. She told the highway drifters, "You do not have the slightest idea of who you are dealing with. You have absolutely no effect on them. Your weapons are as toys in comparison to what they possess. You must leave immediately, I believe you are making a big mistake. For the sake of life, please do not make a direct movement toward one of them, for I do not know what they are capable of. I have seen their strength and power. I tell you, it is not pretty!"

Urvenus opened her cloak slightly as she laid her hands on some kind of weapon.

Two of the robbers rushed for Urvenus, but before they could lay a hand on her, a long sharp sword was extended remotely from a battle gear on the forearm of Uriel, coming to a perfect stop just one inch away from the face of these thieves.

Uriel said nothing, standing almost two feet taller than these robbers. He simply retracted his weapon by tapping a small remote button on his forearm's battle gear. He placed his index finger from both arms on the chests of these men, causing their feet to become partly frozen for a few seconds. Removing his fingers from them, Uriel made their feet return to normal. It could have been much worse for these men, but it was simply for them to beware of who they would meet on the roads, robbing more people.

Tandoor was nervous, for she thought Uriel was going to kill these men with his weapon. She held her chest as she took deep breaths, for those thieves were some of the worst there was in that part of the country.

Urvenus stood still and didn't even have to move a muscle. The threat was light for a heavy response.

"Mr. Uriel," said Tandoor, "has there ever been a time in which emotion overtook your intellectual knowledge to create space for something other than your present activities?"

Uriel answered, "If you are directing your question to an emotional state with an opposite gender, know that we were all created by the same source. The difference is but social and intellectual levels of an abstract life source and advanced technological engineering, which is based on different levels and universes. Therefore, a human of this earth can in no wise commit in existence with a higher creature from an outside world other than your own. A mutual agreement and understanding would not exist."

Tandoor understood very little about what Uriel said.

CHAPTER 7

Awhile later, they arrived at the town of Alsace. There, the center of attraction was all theirs. Some folks were a lot curious about what a young girl was doing roaming around with these two warriors. A noble man stopped them and said, "On behalf of all, we give you thanks in your efforts to set our country aline, for our people have been in chaos for a long time, and no one has shown concern."

Urvenus walked up to this kind man, held his hands in hers, and placed a wonderful pendulum made of a strange material that could not be found anywhere on earth. Urvenus said to this man, "This is a reward for your gentle and noble behavior for a lifetime of doing good to all your kind. This ornament will be a protection for yourself and family and sha also bring you closer to your maker."

The man was so glad that he wept, for these two extraterrestrials were the only ones that had ever treated him with affection. His wife was an alcoholic, much involved in adultery, as it was said that he was destroyed emotionally by his own spouse that he became insane. For more than forty years, he never spoke to anyone, for the pain and suffering he endured was too much to bear, as he loved his longtime childhood friend very much, later becoming his wife. Most of his days he spent near a beautiful lake, to be at peace and feed on spiritual concentration. His name was Boris Iluvious. His two young children, Arnold and Trina, both in their midtwenties, were brutally murdered by bandits nine years ago. Since then, a sister that he never thought was alive came to his side one year after he lost his beloved children. His wife was lost in perdition long ago. in perdition long ago.

As Uriel and his company were about to move on, Boris stood in front of them and asked them not to leave just yet, for he wanted to take them somewhere. Uriel already knew where Boris wanted them to follow, so he nodded his head in agreement.

Tandoor followed closely behind, for she enjoyed being around Uriel and her friend Urvenus, earlier known as Clare.

They walked on through a beautiful meadow where cattle grazed on fertile green savannahs. This part of the region was doing great in terms of survival and healthy land.

Boris was a little sick. When he walked, his left feet would drag on the ground as if unable to move up and down, becoming tired very quickly.

Uriel gazed on the strange-looking creatures on four legs, eating the grasslands, for where he came from, they did not exist. He also kept an eye on Boris, who was about sixty-five years of age.

A short while later, they arrived at the place where Boris was taking them. It was the lake where he would always go to enjoy nature. The crisp blue waters riddled in tiny waves as the wind blew into the trees.

Uriel went and stood next to the lake, seeing his reflection wiggled in the water. He unlocked a small mechanical tool, the size of a telephone earpiece, submerged it in the water, then took it back out, and looked closely at a small screen on the face of the instrument. Clearly, he was examining the water, perhaps for poison or other types of hazardous gasses. While doing this, his other arm was pointing out toward the entire lagoon. A steamy substance shot straight out of a padded material located on the very palm of his hand, but not reaching the water. Just after doing this, he closed his hands together, and the strange steamy substance faded.

Boris and Tandoor asked Urvenus what was Uriel doing with the e water. She replied, "On a certain territory on our planet, most stagnant liquid on the ground's surface contains high levels of methane gasses and sulfur acids, lethal to any form of living creatures. Some of our species on Sedna have the resources to cleanse all dangerous chemical in hydrogen dioxide liquid, or water as you call it. Uriel is one of them who possesses this ability. Even though he has remained on planet earth for a very long time, he has never trusted some things of creation, for many secrets of danger lie hidden before your very eyes yet cannot be seen with the naked eye!" Urvenus loved the great outdoors and enjoyed the place where Boris had taken them.

Boris had told them that he found tranquility and a peaceful state of mind at this certain location.

Uriel asked this old man, "Why is it you seek this comfortable atmosphere and isolate yourself from the rest of your earthly comrades?"

Boris answered, "There is too much corruption and disgrace in the lives of many of us." The pain and sorrow could be seen in his eyes when speaking about this matter. "Therefore, I come to this place of mine to ask our Almighty Creator to help us all and forgive our sins. There are moments when I feel as if he has forgotten us like those helpless people in Lorraine."

An old oak tree with termites stood nearby. Next to it was another tree, very healthy looking with green leaves and thick branches.

Uriel went up to the healthy tree, broke off a single branch with a leaf on it, and said, "This branch is from a healthy tree on which no termites tread. Notice the leaf on it is very alive." He then said to Boris, "Hold it and try on breaking it."

Boris did as he was told. He tried very hard on breaking the branch of about one inch in diameter. He applied much pressure but was unable to crack the thin branch and handed it to Uriel.

Tandoor was staring on at what Uriel was demonstrating but understood nothing.

Uriel then went to the old sick tree infested with termites and broke off a branch much thicker than the previous one from the healthy tree and gave it to Boris and said, Now intend on breaking this branch from this tree.

Boris held it and broke it easily without any pressure. Boris then said, "I can see that one is easier to break than the other, but I don't understand what a tree has to do with people."

Uriel replied, "Both trees are a creation of the one who is in control of all, yet one is weaker than the other. Both trees are just as two men, both created by the same source. The old tree is as a man who has deprived himself of all that is glorious; the termites are the evil thoughts and actions that are followed by sorrow. In contrast, a branch from a healthy tree, even thinner, could not be broken, equal as a man with pure and noble actions throughout his life shall live without pain and grief, for he has never been infested with termites. It lies in him to rise for what he was created. Your neighbors in Lorraine are a consequence of what surfaces when many people deprive themselves of what is noble."

Boris understood vividly of what was said to him.

Tandoor looked at Uriel as if she wanted to throw herself and hug him, for his calm and gentle explanation was so touching and understanding.

Urvenus slightly bowed to her brother in respect, as she admired his rank given to him by elders on their home planet.

Uriel was pleased with his newlyfound friend, Boris.

Urvenus was right by his side should he lose balance and fall to the ground.

Boris had erected a small hut on a little hill beside the lake, despite he had a small home in midtown. Boris asked Uriel if on his homeland there were trees and grass fields with beautiful meadows.

Uriel said," You have much to cherish, my friend, for we have not been so fortunate on our world. Centuries raged on for a very long time against other species. Fields of fertile land were lost to radiation from enormous explosions. Among our hard target was your world. Although not a full contact with earthlings, their backlash of negative activity creates poison gasses, tearing an unseen layer of protection, shielding your kind from self-extermination. In this process, toxic materials flowing far beyond your reach into the vast universe cause friction between our galaxy, Trifid Nebula, and your own Milky Way; therefore, our retaliation must carry on. On Sedna, our comrades now exist in cooperation and peace with many other species from distant worlds. It is the only way for survival in an advance world for a harmonious and healthy environment, one which your people will in time reach. As for the results, you can see for yourself as we both stand here before you."

Now have in mind that the reason why Uriel told this to Boris was so that faith for doing what was right was not lost for this old man.

Boris placed his hand on the shoulder of Urvenus and said that it was time to return to the city of Alsace where he lived. On arrival at the home of Boris, his loving sister greeted him. He told her what wonderful beings he had met. They both said goodbye to Uriel, Urvenus, and Tandoor, who was still hot on their heels.

CHAPTER 8

As they left the city, they came across a cemetery. Uriel stopped and entered along with Urvenus.

Tandoor was somewhat jittery about entering, for she knew it was forbidden to enter without permission from the keeper.

Urvenus and Uriel had never been in a place quite like this. Urvenus looked around in wonder staring at so many monuments all in rows very much alike.

Uriel stooped slightly to read what was written on a grave. When he ended reading, he slightly stepped backward and stared at the grave with extreme focus. His sight was so powerful that he penetrated the concrete. He saw nothing but human bones in and beneath those graves. His reaction to what he saw was a little strange, as he moved his head slightly to the right then to the left as if trying to understand why bones were hidden inside a concrete box in a large open field. He then asked Tandoor, "These sepulchers, do they all contain human remains, or are they also built for rituals?"

Tandoor answered, "They all contain deceased bodies of many people who were said to be evil in nature, those who practiced witchery, along with regular citizens as well. This is where mankind is laid to rest. Don't you have a place like this on your planet?"

Uriel replied, Indeed, but not as yours, for ours are stored in transparent shields suspended above ground, kept in constant observation. Some of which are regenerated then modified for special duties."

According to Tandoor, this was a graveyard where many dangerous people were buried.

Urvenus knew there were cemeteries but had never stepped in one. Uriel, however, spent most his time in the far and remote locations, away from most human contact.

As the day rolled on, a storm was brewing on the horizon. Lightning and thunder exploded high above in the clouds. Uriel, Urvenus, and Tandoor exited the graveyard they visited and headed for Lorraine, which was about six hundred miles away. It began to rain as the three friends made their way outside this fertile city.

Tandoor stopped and stated that she could not continue any longer due to her earthly lifestyle. She said there was some business she needed to take care of in that city. Tandoor warmly embraced her friend Urvenus. She then gave two steps forward and looked up at Uriel and laid her hand on his cloak and said, "You are both wonderful beings, and I shall see you again."

What Uriel and Urvenus had in mind was unclear, but they were a bit eager to get to Lorraine.

It was pouring rain in that evening but didn't seem to bother these two folks. As they walked through the rain, in just a second, they had disappeared.

Forty-eight hours later, they reappeared on the borderline of Lorraine and another town. They both stood facing what was once a beautiful place.

Uriel detected the presence of Von Seth once again, but this time it was a little late.

Urvenus fell to her knees slowly as a sharp hatchet had buried itself into her back. The deep gash was visible on her, but there was almost no blood as we were all used to seeing. She appeared to be of flesh and bones, but from within her body, rather than blood, there was just a bright glow of light that could be seen through the wound.

Uriel could not see Von Seth, for he was gone instantly. Instead, about a dozen hooded knights confronted Uriel.

They were of the kind that was exterminated almost one month ago in Ireland.

Urvenus was injured badly but was not dead. There was no painful reaction on her beautiful face, but she was losing strength slowly. She fell face-first into the ground with tears in her eyes. Suddenly, the hatchet seemed to have evaporated, for it simply vanished from her back.

The druids drew closer to Uriel, but he paid no attention to them. He was concentrating on something else. He placed three odd-looking objects into the ground, and a glassy electric sort of shield appeared around Urvenus. The reason for this shield was unknown, but Urvenus could be seen through it lying on the ground.

These knights were sent surely by Von Seth, who was the first to attack but could not be detected or seen by Uriel, for he left in a split second.

Uriel had a bit of anger in him, for volts of electricity could be seen on his fingertips. A few local citizens approached but retained their distance because of fear.

Just a few yards away, the murderous knights stood staring at this beast, thinking he was outnumbered, as they slowly surrounded him, forming a circle around him from which there seemed no escape except to fight and win.

Urvenus appeared to be sleeping inside the shielded cover, unknown if she was still alive. The glassy shield at moments glowed fiery red then would diminish and become transparent once again.

The druids were concentrated on destroying Uriel. Little did they know their efforts would be in vain once more, just as in Ireland.

As Uriel turned around while in one place preparing himself for battle, two knights moved violently toward him but were stopped in their tracks by the massive hands of Uriel. Each was held by the collar as in a choking claw. The two druids could not break free. They were lifted right off their feet into the air. While grasping for air, a light crunching sound was heard as their necks were snapped like a toothpick. These two knights were killed instantly and simultaneously. Their bodies were dropped to the ground heavily by Uriel.

Another knight attacked with a sword but found himself disabled, as his feet seemed stuck in one place. Uriel had paralyzed his mobility. That powerful weapon on the upper shoulder of Uriel was activated, moving from left to right as if scanning its target.

The druids decided to leave but would not escape, as Uriel fired multiple beams of lightning from that awesome weapon. It had hit its targets. All nine remaining killers were vanquished instantly, as they all seemed to have been blasted into nonexistence.

A polished metal object was in the hands of Uriel. He pointed it at the two bodies on the ground, as a bright beam of red light erased the two knights, who would never be seen again, as well as the last one who was unable to move.

The fight was over, but Urvenus remained inside that shield, very injured. Some people, standing near, moved toward Uriel and asked if he needed any assistance. A young woman of about twenty years of age said, "She seems as an angel asleep, yet I see her almost lifeless body taking in oxygen heavily and further apart," for both she and Uriel required a portion of pure air to exist on earth, perhaps on their planet as well.

The objects that were placed into the ground were removed by Uriel. They looked like glass stones, or diamonds if you will. The glowing shield around Urvenus disappeared right away as she stood on her feet. She held her brother by the hand and said, "I truly thank you for your assistance and remaining beside me, but most of all, my beloved brother, your accomplishments sure come in handy at all times!"

The young woman standing next to Uriel looked at him in awe, with her eyes wide open, and said, "I see with certitude that you possess the ability of returning the dead to life. How did you, sir, acquired this gift?"

Uriel answered, "Your comment has no keen of understanding, for you see only as far as your eyes can see. Our technology, as you shall call it, in healing, is just as your medicine and your doctors in whose hands would lie a sick one as he intends on revitalizing and aiding the natural healing of the human body.

What I have used, as you can see, is a method of saving a specie of my kind, but if her time was on her, nothing would have saved this hollowed body. As for the matter of life and certain death, it is reserved for the lord of all lords who created all forms of existing creatures, including the vast universe and its planets."

Urvenus told Uriel, "We must enter this thorn land and strive to succeed in uplifting the habitation standards of these deprived souls."

They entered Lorraine once again and made their presence known among the Forgotten 44. The streets were filthy with debris and human wastes. Some of these folks were so lost that a need for a proper rest room was not needed anymore, neither the use of clothing.

Urvenus and Uriel drifted along as dozens of these mentally sick people followed them wherever they went. A deranged man, almost looking like a beast, ran and sprung unto Uriel from behind, but before the lunatic could land on this large warrior, he was pushed back about fifteen yards away landing right back on the ground almost losing consciousness. Uriel stopped and went back to where the man was on the ground, picked him up, and whispered something in his ears.

The filthy man simply walked away looking back every after few steps he took, thinking that he was being followed. His death came shortly after. No one knew what he was told, but his death had something to do with that whisper in his ears by Uriel.

A few moments later, they came across where Leena's castle was situated, whom—as we might know—later was known as Celine. As they stood on those grounds near the outskirts of Lorraine, they heard a voice that sounded like angels singing from every side, for it was their mother getting in contact with them from far away. Uriel and Urvenus stood still, while concentrating, as a cool wind around them.

For the first time ever, there was a slight happy reaction on the face of Uriel on hearing his mother's voice. Urvenus had a light smile on the face. This incident lasted just a few minutes and was over.

What was said to Urvenus and her brother was not known. Their communication was telepathic.

They both left at that moment. Moving through some old, unoccupied, and abandoned part of this forsaken town, Uriel came to a sudden halt and instructed his companion to follow behind him and enhance her battle gear, for something was not right.

Von Seth was spotted by Uriel about a mile ahead, in between some broken-down buildings. Even as darkness was drawing near, with just under an hour left of daylight, Uriel could see his nemesis very well from a long distance. He told Urvenus that Von Seth was visible but wasn't aware that he was being seen.

Urvenus could see the image of this shape-shifter but could not see what he was doing. She asked, "What is the present activity of this evil entity?"

Uriel replied, "Dressing himself with bones of human corpses from a recent kill, marking his territory of victory with the blood of an earthling. I do say it shall soon differ from what it seems unto his eyes. Let us proceed, for Von Seth's time has come."

There was no one near that certain part of town, so a full-scale war could take place. The closest people were about ten to twenty miles away. If anyone were to arrive close by, they would be killed in the middle of battle.

Something unbelievable happened. Uriel held Urvenus by the hand and became unseen as they disappeared into nothing instantly.

A few moments later, they reemerged with an explosion, becoming visible just some feet away from Von Seth. He was a bit shaken due to the sudden appearance and thundering explosion, for he did not expect that Uriel and his companion could stealth themselves and get so near without being seen. Von Seth growled and created a wretched, disturbing noise that would burst the ears of a human but didn't have much of an effect on his enemies.

Uriel walked toward Von Seth, whipping up a huge windstorm with pieces of debris blowing throughout the air, hitting Von Seth very strongly, lifting and pushing him against a tall concrete wall, breaking it into pieces.

Von Seth returned at the blink of an eye before his opponent as if nothing had happened, snarling those fangs like a hungry wolf. His eyes were wide open, turning red, like that of a demon. He ferociously attacked Uriel, but as he did, Uriel rose into midair.

As Uriel did, he pulled out a long sword attached to his arm with a strange design. Coming down for a landing, he wounded Von Seth, cutting the head in half. But only ashes was scattered instead of blood. He was injured pretty badly in his own way, for he moaned in pain with both halves of his head falling apart. This beast was able to insert his hatchet hand into the upper chest of Uriel in the middle of the fight.

Since Von Seth was hurt, dust and ashes poured from his wound. Von Seth was replenishing and renewing himself slowly but surely, since Uriel was also injured.

Uriel had a large hole punched into his shoulder blade area but was still down only to his knees.

Urvenus stood with no fear like a fierce hunter. She launched something that looked like a motorized disk with a very fine razor-sharp cutting blade around the perimeter. Its velocity and brilliance was amazing as it was fired. This dangerous weapon grazed the left side of Von Seth around the rib area, not causing much damage, but a bit of dust still came out of this small wound.

Von Seth fell to the ground, for he already had two injuries on his mutilated body and somehow lost a great deal of strength. Apparently, his inside body was nothing but black dirt instead of blood. Within this dire were found tiny molecules that feed him energy. When he would lose them, he would be out of action, until he regenerated himself.

Uriel was also down but certainly not out, for his wound was very strange as well. His body appeared just as that of a human but very different from the inside, for his energy did not appear to rely on a pounding heart. He was losing strength slowly as he had fallen to both knees with very little expression on his face. It was very confusing to look at his internal body functions, for it was as if he was just a reflection of an angel. It was difficult for the most intelligent human in this era to understand how this creature could survive without internal organs, just as Von Seth could. Uriel was dying very slowly, for he was injured by that of a powerful evil being, even though he seemed so invincible. Let us be aware that these two extraterrestrials were trying to destroy the most powerful evil entity that hell itself rejected, brought to life by centuries of humanity's wrongful actions and aggression against one another and their own planet.

Nightfall had set in, and Uriel was dying little by little. Urvenus did not have the capability to save him. She held her brother in her arms as tears fell from her beautiful blue eyes, looking around as if awaiting for someone to help her. After all, she was only about eighteen earth years of age. Being very caring to her own kind, she said to Uriel as he showed a great deal of strength, "I know you are strong, and you will not allow this wretched creature to eliminate you from existence. Remember, we are created by him who has lost no battle, for his power and might reigns on all his creatures and their galaxies. His armies are perfect in action and can be withstood by no one and by nothing. Now rise, for we were made as a part of his plan and engineered by his wisdom! The lesser human nature we carry on behalf of our father has been deactivated long ago. He was a failure, and his bad influences are no longer with us but that of our beloved Celine." As Urvenus said the name of Celine, she repeated it once more, "Celine. "

Suddenly, a brilliant and powerful ray of light descended from the heavens, directly from in between tall buildings, lighting up the sky. It struck Uriel right on the upper chest, almost over his massive injury. In just a few seconds, it was gone, vanished from ground level, directly up toward the heavens. The strange thing about this beam of light was that within its bright rays, another human-looking creature-extremely small in stature, dressed in pure white-could be seen riding the lightning and inserting something into the body of Uriel, creating an even brighter glow of colored flashes surrounding all three of them. It was difficult to see where this small individual went due to blinding rays from this mother laser's strike.

Uriel rose to his feet very alive, with a steady flow of electricity crackling on his fingertips. His eyes became totally white, standing very still, perhaps communicating with his home planet, thanking his peers on Sedna. Based on what Urvenus spoke while her brother was dying, it seemed that they too were a creation from the same creator that created humanity, simply with a different mechanism from that of the human creation, with a certain task on their world, just as us. This might be a breakthrough in understanding why Uriel and his species were made of different elements and organisms from that of the human creation. It appeared as if the Almighty had always had a plan for all that he made. Perhaps the same agenda, but the road taken by our people had constantly been the wrong one, unlike that of Uriel.

Von Seth had been since long gone from the scene of the battle, yet small bundles of ashes and dust could be seen on the ground. It was still not time to extinguish Von Seth, as it seemed not to be an easy job for these extraterrestrials. The time would soon come to put Von Seth out of his misery, although the time was not precise.

The next morning, there was something very different on the territory of Lorraine. The gloom and dark clouds that remained stagnant overhead for a very long time were gone. The sun broke through, lighting the entire land. There was not a cloud in the sky, as all the residents of this forsaken town looked around in suspense. Even being mentally affected, they could see that something was different.

Now have in mind that previously, Von Seth was injured by the army, as he went down in a hale of bullets, returning quickly to his feet. At that time, the sun broke through, and the gloom was gone but came back when Von Seth rose to his feet. It was not certain, but something very similar was happening.

Overnight, Von Seth was almost put out of action permanently, for he was injured severely. Now, the atmosphere was normal, although the land of Lorraine was still dry and filthy, just as its occupants.

It seemed as if when Von Seth was wounded or incapacitated, it had a visible response to the atmosphere. The outcome of this place was not yet known, but clearly it had a direct link to this shape-shifter, almost as if he was in control of this town, feeding on these ridiculed residents, who were even involved in sexual behavior in the wide open. Something else was happening. Uriel and Urvenus were gone from the face of the earth, for there was not even a trace of their whereabouts.

Five days had passed since that night in which both warriors were wounded. Slowly, those awful dark clouds returned along with a foggy gloom, as if a thunderstorm was closing in, as cries of despair from people were heard throughout the entire town. It was almost fourteen days that those two heavenly creatures were not seen. The few friends they made while on earth were sad because they were not able to say goodbye; however, it was not known if Uriel and Urvenus were gone permanently.

Von Seth continued his rampage, not only in Lorraine but in neighboring towns such as Alsace, where Boris Iluvious resided. He was also spotted on two occasions in Providence, searching for anyone who was of a wicked nature, but folks there were well respected and very wise. Von Seth never returned to this place.

The army rolled into the town of Alsace for unknown reasons. Folks in this city were still in control of their lives but were slowly losing it to the influences of Von Seth. On this faithful day, this angel of darkness was spotted standing in the middle of the road, entering the city of Alsace.

Boris was very ill, but astonishingly, his wife-who had fallen to perdition-gave up her filthy lifestyle and had returned from the dark side.

Delylah was a woman of good nature now, as she devoted her time on making the short life span remaining on her husband very glorious. Boris still held his precious gift on his collar with much pride, even as his health deteriorated day by day.

Time was passing on, and Uriel was nowhere to be seen. Now, Von Seth was unstoppable, for he was determined to making this part of the now-European continent his own hell.

CHAPTER 9

One evening as Delylah was medicating her husband, loud cries were heard on the streets. Everyone was yelling, "The devil! The devil! It has someone on the streets and is about to kill her."

It was Tandoor Von Seth had in his claws, ready to dismember her. He wore a rising black hood over the head now, since it was sliced right down the middle by Uriel. He still had that dangerous hatchet stuck to his arm. It was later known that this weapon he carried was infected with something legends called asufre, Latin, meaning sulfur, scent of the devil, or gunpowder. It appeared as if he was threatening someone to come forth and face him. Surely, it was a call to Uriel and Urvenus, although these two beings had vanished for almost a month.

Just when Von Seth was about to insert his horrible axe into the fragile body of Tandoor, she was zapped instantly from the claws of this beast. Unknown where she was taken, it was as if she was pulled through time into another dimension. Von Seth was a bit puzzled, looking around, trying to figure how was it possible for this girl to be taken from him so easily.

Since this was taking place near the house of Boris, even ill, he stepped out to see what was the situation. He almost fainted when he saw Von Seth, holding his chest and breathing heavily. He wept when he saw great fear on the faces of his people. He held tightly the ornament Urvenus had given to him and said, "My dear friends, in this time of need, why have you forsaken us? We are in need of assistance only you can offer. You rely on a technology given to you by the one Alpha and Omega, ruler of the entire universe, due to your peaceful existence. Come forth and save my people facing death, for you will not fail!"

Shockingly, three massive beams of laser hit the ground a short distance from Von Seth.

A tremendous shock wave was felt, as Uriel had returned along with Urvenus, and in between stood Tandoor, smiling with gladness, even though she was almost killed by Von Seth moments ago. These awesome warriors from a distant world stood about fifty feet away from this killer demon.

In great wonder, the large hole that was punched on Uriel's chest by Von Seth was there no longer. It had disappeared.

Von Seth moved toward his enemies, literally gliding through the air without his feet touching the ground, with fire in his eyes, and stopped even closer to his rivals.

Uriel saw too many people looking on as usual to see what was going to happen. He waved his right arm forward, from left to right. As he did this, an invisible barrier sort of transparent glass was erected, shielding all the onlookers from great danger.

A few folks tried running through this giant wall but were simply bounced right to the ground with nothing more than a few red spots and bruises. These humans were separated from certain death, even though it looked as if nothing protected them.

Boris was near, but Uriel decided to keep him outside this barrier. He had his mouth wide open, breathing heavily and barely keeping his eyes open as he tried to stare at the people behind this invisible perimeter. He sat his supportive walking stick down to the ground. Being inquisitive, he picked up a little rock, aimed, and threw it at another elderly man standing behind this shield, but as the rock was thrown, it sprung back hitting old Boris right on the forehead. He held his upper eye area in pain, as a red lump was formed around it.

Urvenus saw what happened and smiled slightly. She commanded Boris to enter his home, as rhe time was finally up for Von Seth to be extinguished.

Von Seth became unseen, but just as he did, Urvenus dispensed something looking like straight line of frozen liquid at him directly from her hands, quickly returning him to visibility. Von Seth returned the attack as he shot a blaze of fire at Uriel, but the blaze of fire was strangely curved backward and returned to Von Seth by a sudden burst of cold wind that Uriel had somehow created.

Urvenus, with lightning speed, moved toward Von Seth and drove a sharp double-edge dagger with a red glow on the base of the blade right into this monster's throat. What this reddish glow was, was unknown. But it had a strong reaction on Von Seth, for he moaned in pain as dust poured from his stab.

Von Seth was losing this battle on his own terms. He shapeshifted into forms of many different humans, perhaps due to all the murders he was responsible for. After a short while, he plucked out the weapon from himself, with which he was wounded, and flung it to the ground. He seemed very angry as he opened chose huge fiery eyes wide open, crunching those awful fangs of his.

Uriel made his first major attack by clamping his large hands around the ragged throat of his opponent, twisting it from side to side in an effort to decapitate him. Von Seth, who was very strong as well yet a little shorter than Uriel, finally broke free after nearly three minutes of fighting to be released. Even though Von Seth was stabbed on the very location where Uriel held him in a choking claw, he still had more than enough energy to retaliate.

This maniac intended on using his deadly weapon that was stuck to his arm, but Uriel pulled out an extremely fl.at and sharp disklike object, connected it to a power device he had carried on his left hand for about four seconds, and fired it at Von Seth, cutting the weapon arm right off from him. This unique disk blade was so awesome that it traveled some fifty yards away, cutting a moderate tree right down to the ground, landing somewhere in the bushes.

This shape-shifter roared like a full-grown lion, for he did not like being beaten by another powerful entity of his own strength, and even greater.

These magnificent weapons used on Von Seth had caused much damage, making the people of Alsace more confident that they would soon be safe. They yelled for Uriel and Urvenus as they watched this death match unfold.

But these heavenly warriors understood not why these earthlings were so enthusiastic about chis massive display of power, for Uriel and his assistant needed no additional support. Where they came from, wars were fought or, rather said, were fought differently.

Tandoor was so frightened to see all chis gore between chese two creatures from opposite ends that she lost consciousness, slowly falling to the ground. Delylah came to her rescue and took her away.

Von Seth had now lost both arms as consequence of battling these creatures from another planet. He vanished for a few minutes but was back for a second round.

With no use of his arms, his source of counterattack was something never thought possible. He was able to levitate and control at his will large pieces of debris scattered on the ground. These debris were used as rockets, as they were shot through the wind at high speed toward Uriel and Urvenus by the power of this demon.

A long wooden pole used to support a two-thousand-gallon water-storage vat, with a weight of one thousand two hundred pounds, was lifted into the air and flung straight toward Urvenus. She never saw it coming, for Von Seth created a distraction behind her, leaving her unaware to what was coming. It crushed into her well-defined body, blasting her right through the stick walls of an old barn house about thirty feet away. No one knew if she survived, but for some reason, Uriel remained still as if he didn't care about his little only sister.

Amazingly, Urvenus reemerged from the rubble slowly, but regaining her strength rapidly, she was still very alive as she stood next to her own kind, face-to-face, with pure evil. Uriel had cold the army general that no arsenal on the earth could destroy Von Seth but said nothing about weapons of their own.

It was time for the ultimate showdown, as Uriel activated that nuclear-type weapon on his shoulder. In every direction he turned his head, so did this futuristic weapon. This thing looked almost like a modern-day video camera used by professionals. Its base of attachment was situated on the left shoulder with two remote or motorized thin rods allowing it to maintain its position mainly about twelve inches from the upper chest of Uriel himself.

Just when Von Seth was getting ready to stir up debris from the ground as he did before, Uriel fired a very bright green-colored laser lightning straight toward Von Seth, causing an enormous explosion on impact. It caused dust from the ground to rise up into the air very high above. Visibility was zero. Von Seth could nor be seen at all. Everyone behind the transparent shield was safe, as it was certainly created to withstand powerful forces of warfare. The shock wave it created was felt some twenty to twenty-five miles away.

The chief commander felt the tremor in his resting place inside the army base. Uriel used his ultra-thermal vision, but since heat was all around, he was not able to locate his target until the dust was gone almost thirty minutes after the blast.

As for Von Seth, he too was composed of heat. Von Seth was nowhere to be seen as the dust in the air was blown away by a regular nature wind. A burnt area with a large bundle of ashes was the only thing visible where Von Seth was standing; there were even cracks on the ground nearby due to the mighty explosion. This mission was accomplished.

The army rolled into town with weapon of their own, including cannons and hundreds of horse cavalry. Uriel and Urvenus stood in the middle of the road with the wind blowing through them, staring on as the army drew closer.

Two escorts accompanied the general before Uriel. He had questions to be responded while the remaining army maintained their distance.

One of the horseback riders fell off his horse due to fainting, for he feared Uriel so much. Another soldier came and picked him up trying to revive him. As he came back to sense and saw he was still in the presence of chis mighty warrior, he ran away leaving his horse behind. This soldier was the very same one who confronted and tried shooting Uriel, but Uriel had the bullet smashed at the tip of his gun barrel.

By this time, Tandoor had regained consciousness asking if her friends were still alive. She was told the battle was over; Von Seth was annihilated, and her friends were very much alive.

As Uriel stood facing the army, he waved his arm in a side-toside motion, removing that transparent shield from all those people he kept out of harm's way.

The chief in control said to Uriel and Urvenus, "We come in peace with some questions to ask you, sir, about what took place here in Alsace. Whatever it was that you did caused some of my men to cake cover, due to thoughts of an invasion. What was the cause for this activity?"

Some locals shouted, "That ugly monster was about to kill a woman and destroy many, if not all of us. If it was not for these brave extraterrestrials, we would not be standing here; I believe you know what I am saying, general!"

The general replied, "I want answers from the prime characters only. What do you have to say, mister?"

Uriel responded, "Outside the forsaken place called Lorraine, you and your comrades were safe. As for us, we saw your actions and effects. We are aware of negative results enduring time for you earthlings to redirect your actions. And we terminated this danger that lurked among you, all, who have no restraint on this wayward beast you, all, created, so that it would not bring forth perhaps another type of menace hiding in the shadows. I am certain, commander, about your knowledge pertaining to Von Seth. He has been exterminated from your world. He has been a creation of malice on other planets as well!"

The commander was confused because of the method used by Uriel to speak, as it was the only way for him to communicate with all people on earth. The top-ranking army man said, "I am well aware about the conflict in Lorraine, but we are powerless to enter into chis place due to mortal infections! I was certain of a bad entity roaming this part of the continent but was unaware it had a name! I shall do all I can to end warfare in this part of the world. Tell me, sir, what have you done with this creature?"

Urvenus, who was listening answered, "Von Seth is and was a very powerful prince of darkness, existing for thousands of years around the universe, on a constant war against the lord of all power and his army on other worlds, now recently on this planet of yours!

As a human does that which is wrong, a tiny microscopic part of this entity is born. At its prime reach, he creates havoc among whoever he wishes, but out of reach he is with a noble one!"

The high chief said, "If what you say is true, we thank you for your support, but there are others who will not take your word seriously!"

Uriel stared at the general and spoke upright, "If you earthlings do not heed our warning, then we shall be forced to extinguish the cause as well as its residue. I have said it once. Your immature conduct generates holes in your atmosphere causing toxic gasses to flow far beyond where humans have not yet reached. This creates a strong friction between our galaxies; this we can't ignore. Our existence shall not be terminated because of your quest for vengeance and wars!"

The high army official was a little offended at the words of Uriel, for he was not the kind of human who enjoyed taking orders from anyone below his rank. Perhaps this army leader felt he was beyond these two heroes. This general was not as respectful as he appeared to be, for he said to his men in a teasing tone of voice, "This insolent believes he can tell me how to operate my country."

Saying this, he and his cavalry rode away on their hefty stallions.

Uriel and his assistant might need to make a difficult decision since they were mocked by this army leader.

Boris was standing, holding his walking aid, next co Uriel, slightly lowering his brow just before he slowly went into his home.

Tandoor walked toward this exterminator named Uriel and tried to put her arms around him but was unable to reach his shoulder. Instead, she simply gave him a timid smile and backed off slowly.

Uriel only stared at her with, of course, more serious problems. He said to his sister, "The seal of damnation over that which is called Lorraine has been broken, and its occupants have returned co sanity from the slumbers of ridicule. This mission is still to be undertaken, for it does not end with the termination of Seth."

What Uriel meant was soon to be discovered.

Meanwhile, at the military camp, the general was plotting to capture these Martians, perhaps to experiment and even revoke their power. To do this, he would need all the help he can gather, for he knew it was going to be highly dangerous. Other highergovernment officials had no idea of what was brewing in the mind of this general, for he was acting alone on this wicked plan. It appeared as if the extraterrestrials had more than just a terrible shape-shifting creature to deal with. The problem was, how should humans undertake an action against someone who was equivalent to the might of three hundred armies?

Uriel had told Urvenus about the general's intentions, but neither of chem seemed to care.

Tandoor told Urvenus that she had something to do in another part of town and left.

A message was sent to the ruler of the French region, saying a miracle had happened. All inhabitants in Lorraine had suddenly started speaking and cleaning up the filch on the town streets, aiding one another and feeling ashamed of their living conditions.

All the dark skies and gloomy surroundings had vanished. Clean and fresh rain fell from the heavens above almost immediately after this transformation took place. People in Lorraine were singing and praising the Almighty Lord, for it was a very long time since they had seen rain falling very heavily on their once-dark city. In just a few weeks, this renewed place was blooming with luscious green gardens and fruit trees.

CHAPTER 10

The governor was a very wise and kindhearted gentleman. He sent a message to Uriel and Urvenus, asking them to come into his presence. Apparently, the governor knew that those two individuals roaming the earth had restored this forsaken town with the help of a supreme being.

Uriel agreed to the request of this man as well as to a plea to speak a little more on where they came from. They were still in the city of Alsace when they were called on. Shortly after they had received the summons, Uriel and Urvenus were gone with the twinkle of an eye, but never went to see the governor.

A few hundred yards away from the home of Boris, a little girl in a group of people kept staring up toward the limitless skies for a great deal of time. No one knew what was happening to her, but it was as if this child of tender years was enchanted by whatever she was gazing on. It was a little cloudy that day, but the bright sun did break through for the major part of the day. All the animals around the outskirts of the city were acting strange as if something was not right, but nobody thought anything else was wrong.

Uriel and Urvenus were gone for almost twenty-four hours but had agreed to visit the governor in time to come. Where could these creatures go when they would vanish for extended period?

That was a mystery that perhaps one day would be discovered.

The following day, around early evening, an earth tremor was felt around the entire French region. Could it be a warning about something wrong about to happen? An hour after the shock, two beams of light made ground contact several miles from a legendary place known as Salem. These lasers seemed to have originated from within the earth's atmosphere. It was Uriel and Urvenus returning from their unknown resting domain, or perhaps even from their own planet several light-years away.

On arrival at the governor's building in central France, a large group of people welcomed them as they made their way to a platform built for them to speak about their presence on earth. This was held in a wide-open backyard of the government building. Everyone stared at them in suspense, wondering if these strange-looking creatures were indeed from another planet. Uriel wore that full-length black combat coat, which was son of his war gear. As for Urvenus, she was similar in wardrobe as well except for a black shawl worn over her head down to about shoulder length with strange markings up on the forehead area and a silver star possibly signifying a data number on her world.

The governor shouted, "Welcome, folks! It is our pleasure to have you with us today. I believe it is you both who restored that wasted town of ours. Your actions are greatly embraced."

Uriel was certainly not accustomed to all these extravaganzas, for there was not a smile on his face neither was there anger. He was simply not a regular friendly man from this earth.

Urvenus said firstly as introduction of themselves, "For many years, we resided among your kind in the town of Lorraine. Our bearer by the name of Celine was sent to your world centuries ago. Although she roamed on every part of the earth, she came to a halt here in this continent now known as Europe. A foundation was extended for Uriel and myself, as an effort to advance this mission without making it known to humans. Celine was terminated at the hands of your military men due to fallible Judgment. This was to happen as it was ordained by higher elders on the core ?f this task; this is why she was exterminated without her retaliation. If we were sent directly to you, all visible to your eyes.' we would most certainly be consumed by critics and explorers in search of the mystique space!"

The governor asked Uriel to speak a little about the unknown. Uriel raised his brow just slightly as if looking for some kind of signal from above. He then spoke, "We are descendants from great legions of the ruler of all creation. We strive for a peaceful existence with creatures from other planets and have succeeded. We acquired an outer human life-form and advanced through an extraterrestrial process. We are patrons from the planet Sedna, pointed out in the constellation of the Trifid Nebula galaxy. This is a world different from your own but with some elements in similarity, perhaps not enough to support human life-forms. That which you called birth takes place, as our species multiply in moderate numbers, although the process is not such as that from a human evolution since we are not composed of internal fluids and working components. To become learned about this, you will need to see the future and submerge yourself in wisdom, which in time you, all, will grasp. I shall say to you for once, it's the angels who trace us. For this, our life span is nearly three thousand years and even longer. Our knowledge of a supreme lord has greatly taught us the manner in which to alter and modify both physical and abstract method of existence. Defense systems and capabilities are strongly engaged to extinguish only chat of a wicked and unlawful nature. A negative surge of energy cripples everything that must prosper. In events of preplanned tragedy, your earth's evolution is shifted into a reverse mode. Unknowingly it creates powerful ripple of unseen danger settling in and outside your world, causing a major problem for they whom you share this endless universe with you, all."

The governor was astonished as he stood with his jaw wide open at what he heard. Listening attentively, he asked Uriel, "Are there more living creatures other than you out there?

Uriel stared at the governor as if the question was too ridiculous to be asked. He looked into the hundreds of people standing near watching and said, "To believe chat you are alone in the universe is as if staring at millions of footprints on a sandy seaside and yet having thoughts of being alone. A constant signal from outside your earth's atmosphere has been active for a long time. This, a powerful source of communication called photons, has been randomly gazed toward the earth. The problem is, your smart men have been looking in the wrong locations or not searching at all, as these message lasers are twisted and scattered across the high heavens due to your planet's magnet protection. This activity displays a colorful horizon on most occasions. It will in time be given a name, but the reality of its origin will have then changed.

The governor said to his comrades to take notes on all being said, for it will sooner or later come in very useful. Most people listening were so glad to hear that they were not alone in the limitless universe.

Uriel also said to everyone, "You, all, shall not live to see the dawn of a new world order but indeed will exist among ones who will bring precious gifts and enable your technology to expand like wildfire. Our knowledge of this is due to our elders' closer understanding and devotion to the maker of the seen and unseen.

As this talk to the people was carried on, a plot was taking place against Uriel and Urvenus by the army general. The talk was finally over, but not before leaving everyone present with gladness, and some even had tears in their eyes to such discovery.

The governor invited Uriel and Urvenus to stay at his home in the capital. These two beings had important matters to deal with, rather than have the luxury of spending a vacation at the governor's mansion.

CHAPTER 11

As soon as they exited the capital city, a heinous trap was awaiting them less than a mile from the city gates. As soon as they left, Uriel ordered his sister to stop, for something was not right. He did not see what was being planned ahead of time due to a scramble in his premonition. Suddenly, this ability of him was inaccurate, and he could not rely on it for the time being.

For the first time, Uriel had somewhat of a concerned look on his face, for someone or something was tampering with a power that would bring death to anyone who acquired it.

As Uriel and Urvenus looked on into the distance, about a half kilometer, around twenty human images standing near seven feet tall were closing in. It was unclear what these things were. They seemed like humans from a distance, but burnt scars could be seen on a fraction of their faces. As they came within fifty yards from Uriel, they disappeared. Uriel could still feel their shimmer in the air and said to Urvenus, "They were powerful warlords from the Wastelands. They have been isolated from their comrades in the underworld and have now been recruited by someone that resides in this land."

The scrambling in Uriel's speedy, forward brain seemed to interfere only on certain moments. These warriors from outside stood on the side of the road during this short moment but walked for a few more yards and vanished into nothing within a second. Two days later, they made their presence felt among citizens in a place called Providence. These people were a little more sophisticated than many others around the land.

As Uriel and Urvenus suddenly appeared the way they normally did, they attracted some attention, although a few people were a bit busier and hardly even noticed the sudden appearance.

Uriel could feel the negative energy in this city as he roamed on some crime-prone main streets. No one would dare to make an assault on Uriel, but what stood in his way half a city block behind him was awesome as Uriel himself. He saw what it was before, even turning and looking. Uriel and Urvenus turned around and were face-to-face with the same creatures that had vanished before them two days ago.

Standing just around seven feet tall, these individuals confronted Uriel and Urvenus. There was no movement of their lips, but they were communicating in telepathic form. If a brawl was to take place on this city street, Uriel and Urvenus were completely outnumbered; but they were all just facing one another with a serious expression on their faces. These individuals who came before Uriel were just as humans but with many scars on their bodies and a strange length of fingernails appearing black in color.

Uriel suddenly backed away in turmoil as he had understood who these beings were. They had the same trace and characteristics found in someone of relation to Uriel. He understood this because these humanoids were the ones responsible for Uriel's scrambling of his mind visions of future events and had remembered there was only one other individual who upheld this ability. This was a cunning situation for Uriel and Urvenus, for they had no idea of what was about to happen. Once more, the ability for Uriel to look into the future was disabled. These individuals, which numbered around twenty, were very powerful.

The general and his army were waiting just outside this rich city of Providence to take action against Uriel as soon as these powerful beings were done with their task.

The power of twenty mind-controlling mutants was too much for Uriel to overcome. In a split second, a large ultra dome of laser lights draining the mind of Uriel was formed directly over him making him weak. He could not defend himself, for the odds were, too many, but telepathically commanded Urvenus to vanish. Uriel was trapped with no exit by none other than his estranged father's henchmen.

Urvenus tried to engage in stealth mode but was being pulled back to visibility by the mutants. After a few seconds of trial, she was free to disappear. No one could trace her shimmer, for Uriel was enabling her to do this with some of the earth, leaving him trapped behind. This dome of laser was composed of hundreds of ultra-shock molecules chat were acquired from out of this world.

Uriel could not break free from the inside, but another powerful entity from the outside could blast him out. Urvenus was not in position to penetrate this awesome shield due to lack of an elder's power.

The army awaiting outside the city gates were advised to move in and do whatever they desire with Uriel. It appeared that the mutants had a wicked arrangement with the one behind this plot, the army general, who told the leader of these beings that he was not ready to exploit Uriel because he did not have the resources to do so but instructed these henchmen to leave Uriel alone inside this barrier until it was time for the general and his army to do as they will. What was the prize for these mutants to carry out this work was unknown, but surely, it wasn't anything of a good nature. It seemed as if the residents in this part of the world had not yet learned their lesson. An eerie feeling was in the air as the earth shook slightly every few days.

The general and his followers left the city of Providence. The individuals who did this to Uriel stood staring at him from outside this unbreakable dome. A short while after, they walked away leaving Uriel completely alone on a desolate city street, with no one in sight but rats searching for petrified food lying around on the ground.

Not long after, darkness had rolled in, and only flashes of laser lights were seen from a distance in which Uriel lay totally helpless. Inside this dome, it looked as if he was in some kind of conversation with someone or something, for he remained in one place, almost in a meditating state.

Throughout this time, Urvenus was nowhere to be found but was probably speaking to Uriel from wherever she was. Suddenly, in the wee hours of the morning, she appeared in front of this unbreakable, shielded prison. Being watchful that no one saw her, she began chanting words in an unknown language. Shortly after she was finished, a strong shot of greenish fog, looking almost as evaporating steam, screamed right out of her hands, hitting the powerful dome. Unfortunately, nothing but a slight interruption in the pattern of flashing lasers happened.

Uriel could be seen through these bright flashes lying flat on his spine as if he was dead, but he chose to do this because in Sedna, any being in distress would always position itself facing upward for a more vivid focus and response from another positive source, or extraterrestrial if you will. Urvenus tried with much effort to make her relative burst out of his confinement but failed on every attempt. Her power was yet too young and of a lower category. After all, she was only eighteen earth years of age.

Three hundred years into the future, depending when she came into existence, would make her well over 318 years of age on their homeland. For this to be real, their planet would be rotating at speed far more greater than chat of the earth, but due to their unique intelligence, they somehow were able to slow down the aging process, yet excluding that they also have a life span thousands of times longer than that of humans. If this would not make any sense, could we then say that God created them long before he created us, thus understanding dearly chat we were simply behind them, learning to live the right way and developing unbelievable technology? If Uriel and his companion traveled three hundred years into the past to carry out this mission stopping at 1806, their years of existence decreased, due to time on their planet, but their knowledge and abilities remained the same as three hundred years in the future from 1806. Three centuries into the future from 1806 would make it the year 2106 presently on their planet, which would mean that we humans were just about one hundred years behind them.

Urvenus had renounced her efforts. She needed to find another way to succeed, even if it meant leaving her powerful guide locked up with no knowledge of what was to happen. Hardly wanting to leave, she shimmered away from where she stood staring at this lighted prison that she could not break.

As the sun rose for a new day, strangely the city streets were

empty for about four city blocks. The army had evacuated the people from that part of the city because no one was to know about their activity. The streets were completely desolate, but there were no signs of the military. Uriel remained inside his prison motionless; at some moments, it almost looked as if he was afloat slightly above ground level.

It was impossible to know if his eyes were open or shut due to the blinding lights of this confinement, unknown on what type of material it was made from. It was becoming noon as the sun was covered behind some natural thick cumulus clouds when another sharp jolting of the earth was felt over a moderate area of the country.

Suddenly, a cavalry of soldiers rode into this city to claim their prize. Even though the general was not seen among chem, surely he was not too far away.

A woman, surrounded by several soldiers, was brought down from her horse to the ground. Her identity was unknown, but she was dressed as a bush woman, or what we call a witch doctor, with odd-looking medals hanging from around her colored, thick, and messy hair. It was clear that she was a human, but a sorcerer with magical powers. It was not uncommon to find people practicing this ancient process, good to learn if it was used for evil.

Uriel was completely complete unaware about what was happening in his surroundings. The question was, why didn't he defend himself in blasting his way out of that power done?

Have in mind that Von Seth was a production of the dark and evil actions of people all over, thus beginning him into existence. Thus, finally when it reached its primal point, he took on a life of his own. In this occasion, if another entity from the same origin of Uriel had gone badly, then he would be facing a force of his own magnitude. If these scarred and long-fingered creatures were connected to Uriel's father in some kind of way, then we might be able to have an idea on why these things had the ability to scramble the power of this mighty warrior. On one occasion, Uriel said that if one from Sedna was to disobey a command, he or she would be deprived from all original rights and left as abandoned and unrecognized by his own species.

They were then called Avisteroids, meaning they were considered from the abyss; few were those that were recovered.

This magical sorcerer approached the prison of lights and took a close look at this almost-defeated Martian, then stepped away just a few feet, and pulled out of a bag a golden-colored box with strange designs on it. She opened it as she called for the power of Uriel, perhaps with the help of evil forces. Slowly, the energy from this captive could be seen evaporating through the laser beams entering into this strange container held in the hands of this cynical witch.

Suddenly, a strong surge of energy was pulled by this magical box and blasted this woman about fifteen yards away directly into a stone wall, knocking her totally unconscious with her golden box shattered into pieces.

The small amount offeree taken from Uriel returned directly to him through the laser walls. This sorcerer had failed, and the general was sure to become upset. Perhaps this general was more interested in that state-of-the-art weapon Uriel carried on the lower part of his shoulder, since natural power from Uriel would be of no use to him. He needed this witch to consume all Uriel's strength so he would never have to be concerned about this extraterrestrial coming after him at any moment.

The army men that brought the sorcerer were very frightened and confused, for they thought that Uriel was about to break his way out. Whatever arrangements the general had with those Avisteroids and this defeated witch was going the wrong way.

It seemed like the general had intentions on being dominant perhaps even against his own people. The Avisteroids wanted Uriel weakened so they would be able to take him out with no trouble, for they themselves wanted control over the earth. It would be another battle in time to come if the general was to become dominant with the power of Uriel, since the Avisteroids were aiming for that very same goal.

The sorcerer, still lying on the ground after half an hour, 'was slammed severely into that stone wall. Soon after the horseback soldiers rode away, they did not want anything to do with Uriel if he was to break loose.

Throughout all this time, the father of Uriel was not seen anywhere, but probably granted permission to his followers to seal his own son behind that awesome barrier. Could it be that this wretched creature from Sedna had no idea that those he wanted to destroy were his estranged family?

It was now the third day that Uriel was incarcerated and vulnerable to danger; he was also weakened slightly, but very much alive. He did not know that these Avisteroids from the Wastelands were in understanding with his long-lost father, for the father himself was classified as an Avisteroid. Somehow, Urvenus had to find a way to release her brother from his confinement.

After an hour, the deluded witch woke up and rose to her feet. She tried to put her magical box together, but it was completely destroyed. She was standing right next to this laser dome. As Uriel had his intimidating black eyes fixed straight at her, she was jolted a little when she noticed he was watching her. Even though the bright lights were blinding, but from a very close range, she was able to see inside this thing. She knew Uriel was unable to get out, so she approached this strange dome and placed her hands just above the rays from the laser lights as she was curious to know what this magnificent structure was.

Uriels memory was still scrambled because of those creatures from the Wastelands there, for he did know what this woman was up to standing right next to him outside the laser prison.

Just as the sun was setting behind some far-off mountain, those from the abyss arrived at the place where Uriel was held a prisoner. The sorcerer was still there and said to the creatures, "Your power does not fail you, I would say, but my absorbing magnetic box is by far too weak to hold this Martian's power. If I intend on doing it once more, I might even be killed in the process; it would be of more significant if you execute this matter on your own." The Avisteroids replied in a ringing, sounding, but understandable voice, "We take orders from no one but our leader. What the general has to offer is of no use to us, for we strive for what we want!"

In a recollection of the past, it was understood that Uriel's father was the leader or master of a group of creatures that looked like humans, walking the land in search for dominion over all else that exist on the earth. Apparently, these mutants were the same that were recruited by the father of Uriel. They were now known as Avisteroids from the Wastelands. Since these creatures were governed by one from the planet Sedna, they too were taught or given the ability to scramble the memory of anyone or anything.

As they stood surrounding the dome prison in which this powerful creature was held captive, they agreed to work together with the sorcerer. They knew that if Uriel was completely drained from all his power, they would become victorious, for their victim would then be exterminated easily. Strangely, these evil beings were not aware that Uriel still had a support from his sister.

Although she was not seen for almost a week, surely she was looking on from somewhere in the shadows and would not let Uriel be destroyed.

Just at this time, the army general rolled into town, along with a small number of armed men. The odds were complete as they stood surrounding Uriel pinned inside this pyramid of lasers.

The Avisteroids had their arms spread wide open as they chanted for evil forces to grant them the strength of Uriel. They were much stronger than the sorcerer, being more than a dozen of them. It looked as if Uriel was now to be terminated.

These Avisteroids were suddenly interrupted by a mother beam of laser that hit the ground, causing even some trees to crack because of the impact. This strike sounded like a massive lightning during a thunderstorm. The creatures from the Wasteland could not continue their ceremony, for they were somewhat confused, as it was the same manner in which their leader would make his arrival.

There was smoke in the air, but as it slowly cleared, Urvenus stood facing these twenty demons. What could she do against such awesome force, being totally outnumbered? The difference was that this time, she was not alone, for none other than Celine shimmered into visibility, causing even the earth to tremble slightly. Let's be aware that this angel living on the earth was shot to death some time ago. How was it possible for her to be seen in pure flesh?

The soldiers that had arrived with the general threw their pistols on the ground and ran away, leaving their headmaster and their horses behind. They didn't want anything to do with this situation.

One of them muttered while running away, "She should be dead. What in the blue heavens has she come back for?"

The Avisteroids stood in one place thinking on what they should do. The general had his legs shaking like a twig in the strong wind as he made a dash for his escape, but Urvenus shot a moderate volt of energy at him with a small metal weapon that was clamped on her forearm. His short and stumpy body fell to the ground face-first, shaking like he was breaking apart even while being on the ground.

Urvenus went up to him and injected two very small and unknown pins into his body, almost looking like typical syringe needles used by doctors. As the needles were injected into this soldier's body, the constant trembling ended, but by then he was fast asleep on the ground, due to the shock affecting his nervous system.

Celine stood motionless, staring at those creatures and the witch standing next to them. Her straight jer-black hair almost covered her entire face. Just her left eye could be seen. The area around them was freezing due to her presence. Those eyes on her could never be forgotten, as it looked like pure crystal, literally flickering visions of different dimensions. Or perhaps they were glimpse of heaven itself. She was dressed in a sort of greyish-colored shawl, covering her shoulders, blending into a brilliance of silver at half body, extending down to ground level.

The Wastelanders were a bit skeptical about who or what this creature was, as they stared at it with much caution.

The sorcerer was about to make a step closer to the Avisteroids for protection perhaps, but Celine rapidly glanced at her with those eerie eyes and paralyzed her entire body, leaving only the eyes on this witch rolling around inside its socket. A sharp ray of blinding green light came directly out from Celine's crystal eyes hitting the sorcerer right on the chest, sending her into oblivion, as she was simply erased from the face of the earth.

Astonishingly, even the bare ground was turning into pure ice all around; steam could be seen evaporating from the mouth of the Avisteroids when they exhale. Celine turned her sight on her only son within his indestructible prison with not enough force to break his way out. Urvenus stood in a bit of suspense, armed to the teeth, with a unique, full grey-color battle gear should those strange long-fingered demons make an attack against her bearer.

Celine was a senior patron on her planet, just one level below an elder. These beings were apparently members of God's army, traveling through time at unimaginable velocity in a quest for peace and tranquility throughout the universe and other dimensions. Should they encounter any form of evil, no matter how potent it was, nonexistent it became, for they were those with ultimate power. Celine herself was magnificent and even of a much greater power than Uriel himself.

The Avisteroids kept their eyes fixed on this unknown woman, since Urvenus had electrocuted the general, and her new aid had erased the sorcerer in a single second. For humans to see the complete face of Celine would perhaps be fatal because of a high resolution in those glassy crystal eyes, accompanied by excess radiant energy.

A short while later, a group of soldiers arrived to pick up their general but came to a halt when they landed eyes on the very same woman they had murdered months ago. A frightening reaction was visible on their faces. One of them said to another, "Can you, all, see her? Or is it that I am losing my mind? This woman has been dead for months. Many of you here were present when we fired shots at her."

Another army personnel shouted, "It is a ghost! It is a ghost! It has returned from the grave to take revenge!"

The third official said in a low tone of voice, "We must leave this place at once. We all shouldn't be here."

Since the general was not a direct threat to these amazing creatures, his life was spared, but he remained fast asleep ground due to an electric shock. on the

One of the soldiers came forth with a horse and wagon to load the general who fainted. As he placed his hands on the body, he started to become solid wood from the palm of his hands up to his elbows. He was able to remove his hands quickly and block these phenomena from spreading over his entire body. This soldier was so scared that he went into convulsions for a minute or two.

This general was probably not to be removed yet, for it appeared that Celine had a different plan for him.

Meanwhile, the Avisteroids, being the most powerful evils present, were focused on Celine, as they tried to scan her memory for awareness of what was to follow.

The army men left in a haste, for they were more concerned about their own safety than that of their general.

Urvenus had no idea what those creatures with half-burned faces were up to, much more what was their interest in her brother.

Celine knew very well who they were. Although they could understand telepathic communication, she spoke for the first time, saying to Urvenus in sort of haunting voice, "These twenty beasts standing before us have been turned away by hell itself, just as your recently terminated nemesis. They were catapulted out from the underworld because of intentions on a hostile takeover of the throne of Damien, the source of all evil. They lost. A midplane known to many around the universe as the Wastelands was their new home, a world held captive by a dimension that has no portals. These you view here before us have been rescued from this certain emptiness by someone you do not know, distant away from you and your brother, but his existence shall remain as a seal on your forehead. His name is Blane Shacks."

The Wastelanders were not able to figure out who this woman was, no matter how hard they tried. Probably that was why they were still present.

Celine, on the contrary, was deactivating their power slowly without them being aware. Being an invisible process, it was not known where all this power was being stored. As far as Celine was concern, these powers belonged on Sedna, or with someone from this planet. Her beloved son was still inside his prison, situated just a few feet from where she stood. He was inside this thing for some time now, as no one had the strength to release him.

Darkness was falling. None of the warlords left, for they perhaps wanted to see if Celine had the power to release Uriel from his high-tension laser prison since it was erected by the same magnitude of power that a creature from Sedna had developed as time passed on.

Blane was responsible for these demons, having this kind of ability. Although he was stripped from all his rights, he was still able to depend on his own learnings. The reason why Blane Shacks remained on earth for a very long time creating havoc just as Von Seth was doing was still not known. Would he suddenly be cast into the Wastelands, along with his breed of creatures? Or was there something else in store for him?

It was time to find out if Celine was powerful enough to destroy the immovable dome of lasers. As she stood in front of this pyramid shape of killer lights, a strong flow of energy was being pulled from above, not believed to be from outside the Milky Way galaxy. This energy was clearly visible, looking the same as heat evaporating from the earth on a very hot day. This source of energy was coming from no higher than two miles above the earth, yet nothing could be seen overhead. Even a number of trees that stood nearby were completely destroyed in just a few minutes because of the strange flowing energy spreading around Celine. Celine had both her arms extended before her, absorbing all the force coming from above causing the earth to quake just slightly as well.

The Avisteroids were backing away slowly with concern on their disfigured faces. As for the general, he was still facedown into the ground sleeping as this heart-pounding phenomena began.

He was being pushed around on the ground: energy increased. as the force of this

This awesome display of power was even commanding the weather to shift, for the winds were blowing away everything lying on the ground.

The Avisteroids were holding on tightly to a steel pole buried deeply into a cement platform. This pole v was used for the torturing of criminals in this part of the land. They would be tied from the arms to the saddle of a horse and from the legs to this sturdy iron pole. The horse would then be whipped causing it to move forward, tearing the victim's arms and legs off. As a matter of fact, a man from that very same city was to be put to death the following day at the pole.

We need to wait and see if Celine wasn't going to be in the neighborhood. Because if she was, no one was going to be tortured, much more killed, since the torturing pole was already broken in half and blown through the air like a missile, due to the force this angel was gathering.

The Avisteroids were pushed and clamped to a wall of an old building half a city block away, all twenty of them. They were trying to fight this powerful aggression of nature caused by Celine. It was useless. They could not retaliate.

Urvenus remained right next to her as they both turned facing the immovable dome. Instantly, when this angel felt the time was right, she moved her hands directly forward releasing a moderate amount of radiant energy toward the dome. This thing was shaking like a twig in the wind but was still standing. As the second attempt was of much greater force hitting the laser dome, it completely turned off the laser lights, totally destroying the inner walls created of a thin transparent material yet stronger than steel. Pieces of this thing were found in other towns and cities hundreds of miles away. Now, Uriel was set free but had his eyes closed as he lay facing the heavens, astonishingly afloat about two feet above the ground.

His mother moved toward him slowly, unseen if she used her feet to navigate since her robe was all the way down to the ground. As she came near him, he opened his eyes and rose to his feet without any help from his hands or legs. His eyes were total black, like a polished marble, staring at nothing, as if another entity was in control of him. Celine waved her almost transparent hand before his face, and Uriel came back into motion, as good as new. Urvenus walked forward to greet him in return; Uriel responded by placing his large hands on his sister's beautiful, lustrous long hair.

Up to eight city blocks were affected by the tremendous power of Celine, with moderate damage to some old structures standing about two miles away. Everything within a mile away from where this ultimate dome stood was completely leveled.

As for the Avisteroids that were present, they had vanished just after the showdown between this angel and the immovable object.

It was dark already, but Uriel did something amazingly incredible. Three metallic objects were taken from a small square brown box from beneath his beautiful state-of-the-art custom battle gear. These things looked like diamonds that could never be found on earth. Uriel gently suspended these things above their heads, rising about ten feet into the air all on their own.

As these three things hovered above, they were lighted, and night was turned into day. Urvenus was slightly impressed, for after all, she was still a young cat, enjoying her generation's gift tracing thousands of years back to the existence of angels in heaven. Uriel then turned toward his beloved Celine, knelt before her in great admiration and respect. He did this not because he was aided to his freedom but because on Sedna, creatures of a higher power and knowledge were respected and honored, for they were the ones who kept the universe at peace and served as guardians on their galaxy. Uriel and Urvenus, along with millions of others, were sent on selective assignments far away from their galaxy to rectify smaller threats.

Uriel was a powerful beast, but not to its primal point, for he was still a young man in earth years, older than Urvenus of course and much more potent. He rose to his feet and gently placed his thumb on his mother's bro and one hand on her shoulder. He was not the kind of individual that would show emotional expression to anyone, but to Celine, it was slightly different, for the gentleness and caring could be seen in his body movement.

No one was in sight for quite a distance, but many people in other parts of the city felt the vibration of Celine's force. As Urvenus stared at her Celine with much love in her eyes, she asked, "Mother, why did you call for support from above?"

Celine replied in her own words, "There is no power on this earth capable of extinguishing my strength, but this abomination against you and your brother is not from a dark source but that from our own kind; hence, the force of a senior patron was not potent enough to extinguish what Blane Shacks and his lost souls intended on Uriel." Celine knew who this Blane was. Apparently, it was not time to bring the truth to surface.

Uriel said to the guardian angel, "Mother, I clung to the hem of your robe when I was younger. You taught me the greatest value of our existence and the pattern in how to coexist with other creatures. I have never displayed my strength over no one unless the reason is brought forth. My duty as an advanced specie is to concur the end of all perdition over everything that is not glorious. I am aware of the presence of him who has failed to his duties. Even as I carry his seal on me, his ruthless aggression against these helpless humans is surely not of consent."

Celine seemed honored, as a brilliant shining smile was seen on her face when she heard her two beloved speaking and uniting with her. She extended her arms toward them and said, "Before I left this plane, I uttered that I would look after you from time to time, never leaving you alone, for my spirit shall remain within you throughout your accomplishments until it's time for you both to return unto us. I shall see you in the future. May peace be with you and your efforts be fruitful!" Celine slowly vanished into thin air. It was as if she was pulled by a force straight up into the heavens, for the radiant energy could be seen rising into the air above.

Urvenus stood next to Uriel as they looked at the debris scattered across a wide area. They were able to see for a long distance because of those diamond-shaped illumined object that Uriel had activated. As daylight approached, he extended his hands, and the objects' bright lights slowly descended to him. He took them and placed them in an inside pocket under his coat.

There was much destruction caused by the awesome power of Celine. Uriel turned a full 360 degrees as he held one hand in front of him. As he did this, everything was restored back to its original place, as if nothing had happened.

The general was gone, but not to another location. Uriel had made him unseen by the human eyes. The soldier was still there at the same place but was simply hidden.

In this part of the land, a place called Providence, many atrocities by human authorities were being committed against other humans, even if found innocent. After all, these people were very fallible and judgmental, eager to show domination to their local citizens. This was how victory was shown by these people-a fight to overthrow the weak so the strong would survive. Humans had their own earth war on a regular basis, for much conflict was seen across the continent.

This was one of the main reasons Uriel was sent to the planet earth, to exhort earth citizens of a dark residue, even greater than its actions. But on some occasions, Uriel and Urvenus had to give these people a moderate lecture of behavior, as they did with the general, some highway robbers, and many more. Have in mind that Uriel and Urvenus had never harmed or killed any human, for that was forbidden by their peers, unless a great threat was presented.

As the sun rose, Urvenus and Uriel were in the same location where the powerful dome stood. It seemed as if they appeared to with a be discussing something, as Urvenus held some kind of weapon monitoring gage that she had removed from her arm. a power It seemed to be connected to her spinal area, perhaps support for weapon control. These awesome machines that these two individuals carried around were constructed three hundred years into the future and on another planet. So imagine, it was of nothing of this earth. It was by far more effective and potent than the one being manufactured in the future on this planet.

CHAPTER 12

Amoment after, loud cries of weeping people were heard coming from the other side of the city. A young man of about thirty years of age was being brought through the streets half dressed and was being beaten with a stick repeatedly across the spine. The cries for help from his wife and children were heard as they asked for help.

Uriel and Urvenus remained where they were, awaiting to see what was taking place in this city. Little by little, the shouts got louder as they came closer. Some other people were cheering on the prosecutors as they surrounded this man probably with the thoughts of executing him. A few minutes later, they were visible by Uriel, coming around the corner, as a large group of local authorities brought this man tied from his wrist as another officer beat him on the back. It seemed as if this man's wife and children were crying for someone to help them, as the authorities punished this innocent human. The officers drew closer to where this person was to put him to death.

The reason for this activity with the city authorities was not known, although the prisoner's wife kept repeating in desperation, "Please, don't do this to my husband. He does not deserve to be murdered. It wasn't his intention of being a witness to their activities. Please, I beg of you, chief. Prevent this brutality from being carried out. It is a direct crime on your behalf."

It was the police chief who was in control of this execution. As these people made their way to where Uriel and Urvenus were standing, they came to a stop, for Uriel and his sister were standing near the spot where their actions were to be done. It was about noon, and little more than a hundred people cheered on the were about to do. We would all just have authorities for what they to wait and see if this would be possible while Uriel was present.

When the prisoner's wife saw Uriel and Urvenus, she knew that these two were the ones whom everyone on the land spoke about.

Uriel already knew why these authorities wanted to execute this poor man. Uriel knew this person was innocent as well as a strong threat for some of the authorities.

As the group of executioners was a couple of yards away from Uriel, one of the officers in charge of the execution declared in a demanding voice directed to Uriel and Urvenus, "We know who you are and wish to have no trouble with you. The emperor has given us the orders to execute this criminal. You must abide by our laws. If you intervene with the work of the government, then the entire weight of judicial court will fall on you."

Uriel and his sister said nothing in response to the words of this lawman but were not at all intimidated. The rest of officers continued beating this defenseless person, as it was getting to the point when the prisoner couldn't move any longer. It was sad to see the very same organization that swore to protect and serve were now the aggressor to the human race. The exact location where the activity was to take place was still a few yards away.

A few minutes later, a large and powerful stallion was brought forth with a rope tied to its saddle extending around fifteen yards behind it. It was understood that a certain pole buried deep into the ground was used for this horrible activity. The individual was tied to this pole by the arms and from the legs to the horse saddle. This was exactly what was to be done to this wrongfully condemned man. The prisoner's wife wept so much that her eyes were swollen, as her two young children cried for their daddy not to be taken away.

Now remember what had happened to this thick metal pole when Celine blasted Uriel out of his confinement. At that moment, everything nearby was completely destroyed, including this so called execution pole. With Uriel's three metallic objects, all that was destroyed was then replaced to its proper position, except for this metal pole.

The officers behind this awful act had already noticed that the execution pole was broken but didn't understand how it was done, because it was as if it was snapped in half without being uprooted. It was paid very little attention by the people in charge of this prisoner, for they simply thought of building another.

The chief officer said, "It is clear that someone or something had destroyed our execution pole, but it shall not disable our orders to carry out this work. He shall be tied to the base of this tree! Now bring the stallion!" This chief officer was now going to use a tree instead of the metal pole. The tree he chose was very thick in diameter.

Uriel remained in a still position along with Urvenus, as their long robe blew in the wind, staring from a short distance at the atrocities that were being committed.

The condemned man was viciously pulled from the hair unto the ground and tied from his both hands to the tree. Another officer held the prisoner's feet and tied them together. Most spectators stood near wondering if someone would interfere in the work of authorities. Uriel and Urvenus were some fifteen yards away from the activity.

The prisoner's eldest son pleaded to Uriel, "Please help us. The power is in you to save my papa. They want to kill him because he knows of a horrific crime that was done by these officers to a decent family a year ago. My daddy needs to die so they can save themselves!"

Urvenus called the young boy of about fourteen years of age and told him not to worry because his daddy would not die.

As the death squad arranged some paperwork needed to complete the execution, the boy grew more desperate. The prisoner asked to speak to his wife for the very last time, but his request was denied with a thundering blow to the head with the barrel of a pistol. About two dozen armed lawmen were at the scene where the believed criminal was to be put to death. It was surely a gruesome sight for the children of this tortured individual, for pools of blood were traced from the doorsteps of this helpless man's home, which was some six kilometers away.

The worst activity of this brutality was that even the residents of this city were shouting angrily for this helpless and innocent man to be torn apart without even knowing the motive why the authorities wanted to eliminate him. After all, these folks did not care for reasons. All they wanted was to see gore and mayhem.

Uriel still up this moment did not bother to move a finger in preventing this wrongful activity. The young fourteen-year-old boy stood just a few feet from him, as he awaited for this distant creature to do something to disrupt this execution. Some of the officers faced Uriel and Urvenus holding their pistols with a finger on the trigger as if they were not intimidated. The paperwork was almost ready, for they were eager to continue with their aggression against this man. Their intentions were to have him dismembered.

The youngster lost hope for this beast to save his father. Uriel already knew very well that this man was innocent and why the local authorities wanted to kill him. The question was, why had he done nothing to stop this abomination? Could it be that he was a coward after all or perhaps he was concerned about the backlash of going up against the most powerful human in this continent? In any way, it was the emperor's wish for the execution to take place, although it was not known if he knew the reasons why this man was marked for death.

As the prisoner's eldest son was about to walk away, he was held back. Urvenus told him that Uriel wasn't going to let him down.

A heavy but mellow voice said, "Little one, you came into my presence to ask for assistance in behalf of no one but yourself. You, my son, are as an oasis in the middle of a forsaken desert, where all but lizards exist. Those ruthless earthlings surrounding your dear father are like the desert that kills without a reason. The spectators are like lizards seeking for food!"

This young man understood what Uriel told him because he was very intelligent, for he was thought by a private professor at his home.

Uriel then asked the boy, "Do you know what is courage?"

The youngster answered, "Yes, sir. It is when someone is not afraid!"

Uriel replied, "Courage is not the absence of fear. It is doing what is right, even in the presence of danger!"

The young boy smiled and chuckled slightly.

Uriel took the young boy's hands and placed a beautiful silver cuff made to be worn around the wrist. This was no ordinary cuff like those carried around by regular humans. He told the young boy to walk straight through the officers directly to his beaten father and place the object given to him inside any pocket of his father's remaining trousers, as this bloody man was almost naked. The boy did just as he was told. No one tried to stop him as he walked with no fear over to his father's side.

Uriel and Urvenus watched closely as he placed his little arms around his daddy's shoulders and carefully inserted the strange object in one of the pockets on his father's clothing. This young boy did not even know what was the instrument for, which was given to him, but he didn't care to ask because he trusted his aid. No one saw what the young son did, for it was done very covertly.

The high chief gave the command, "Bring the stallion and tie his feet to the saddle!" As soon as this was said, a very strong deflective force originating from the injured prisoner suddenly some twenty feet away at 360 degrees around him, including the horse that was pushed everyone and everything ultimate and deadly punishment. brought for this

Every man and woman present became extremely frightened as they all looked at one another, wondering what in the world just happened. Some elderly spectators were even blown to the ground due to the awesome outflow coming directly from the wounded individual. Anyone or anything that came near him would be pushed away with a strong force.

Even so, the chief and his lawmen attempted to continue the execution, but their efforts were in vain. The authorities paused for a short while as they tried to figure out what was wrong. A fearless lawman with a nasty character tried to force his way toward the injured man, who was still on the ground. He was able to get to his victim, but on touching him, he began to quiver severely. The veins in his body began to stretch like a rubber. It was also swelling very rapidly, in danger of bursting, causing unstoppable bleeding. This individual was twisting his body in pain, screaming for help, but no one touched him. Suddenly, his eyes burst out of its socket, and the enforcement officer fell dead on the ground.

Everyone stood in great shock because of what they saw. By now, all the yelling for the execution to take place had completely ended due to this strange and frightening phenomena.

Even the high police chief was scared, for his legs were shaking. Most people, who were eager to see the show of blood, ran home in a haste. Some folks thought the man who was to die was a sorcerer because of all this abnormal activity.

Slowly, the injured man rose to his feet, very much in pain due to the beating he endured at the hands of his aggressors.

The high chief stared at Uriel and Urvenus, nodding his head with a vengeful look in his eyes. Perhaps he knew that the extraterrestrials had something to do with what had just occurred. It was obvious that the strange object the boy placed in his father's pocket was the source of this activity.

Going back into the past, when Uriel was in Ireland battling mercenaries that were sent by Von Seth, he awarded another youngster something very similar as the one he gave this boy in need to save his father. The beautiful object was some kind of magnetic shield that would protect anyone it was given to from physical abuse.

As the injured man's vision cleared, he opened his arms to his wife and children. They all ran to him to be reunited in much love and happiness.

The authorities quickly sent a telegram to the emperor, informing him of what had happened, with hopes that reinforcement would be sent quickly. In the minds of these authorities, this family man, whom they knew was a strong threat to them, must be killed at any cost.

For the meantime, the life of this husband and father was spared. The wife of this man whispered something in his ears, most likely concerning the two strange individuals standing in one place throughout the entire activity.

When the rescued man felt the object in his pocket, he took it out and looked at it very carefully. His son said to him, "Father, that man standing over there gave it to me. He told me to place it in your pocket. That is why those gangsters could not harm you!"

It was becoming late by now as the sun was setting. Uriel and Urvenus moved over toward the man and his family. When they came within just a few feet away, the wife said, "I don't know who you are, but I believe you are the two individuals whom everyone speaks about. They refer to you both as visitors from the unknown. You both have done good things for many people. Whatever you did to save my husband, I thank you for keeping our family together!"

The officials were looking on from a distance, wondering what was said between their victim and the visitors from the unknown. After a short while, they left, for they were not able to continue their work.

The injured family man extended his arm for a common greeting, but there was no response from Uriel, for he was not accustomed to this regular way of introducing himself. He was in isolation for a very long time, far away from people; after all, when he was known as Indrid Cole, he spent most of his time in secluded parts of the European continent. The rescued man slowly pulled his hand back, wondering why he was not responded properly.

Urvenus did embrace the greeting and said, "He is not accustomed to a regular introduction. He has been away from human contact for most of his existence on this earth!"

Uriel pointed a faint orange laser light at the wounded man, moving it from the head to the ankles, allowing the man to regain his strength rapidly. No one knew what was the laser for, but apparently, it could help heal the human body. This amazing thing looked very much like a horseshoe as it dispensed laser energy from both ends. The family was so amazed at what Uriel did that slowly they all went down on their knees to render adoration to the visitors from the unknown.

Suddenly, Uriel said, "Rise to your feet now, for I am not who you think I am. An unforeseen future has nestled somewhere in time, a future for success and dignity. We are but only its shadow, trusted into a far-off world, yet of the same source that created you. Our capability is simply altered and modified far beyond your own!"

The former captive were speechless and somewhat confused as it was difficult to understand what Uriel meant. Apparently, a much brighter future was on its way for the human race, one that would allow men of the earth to see beyond their own city gates.

Uriel told the husband and father that with what he was given, nothing and no one could ever harm him again. As nightfall was setting in, the streets of Providence became empty after a day of chaos. The visitors from the unknown bowed slightly, walked away for a slight distance, and vanished into thin air. What these two extraterrestrials wanted was simply for injustice and cruelty on the earth to cease.

To this point, it was still not known where these creatures went every time they would disappear. Although they were able to travel at great speed, it was believed that they resided in the shadows of the night.

After two days, Uriel and his assistant were seen once again in the renewed city of Lorraine, observing the standards of those affected by the terrible famine and its destruction. Now that all darkness was turned into brightness, this once-ravaged city now bloomed with great life.

The residents were now becoming more self-sufficient and intelligent. The streets were tidy and sanitized, along with fields and pastures generating food and wealth very quickly to residents. On one of the city's most congestive streets leading to the city square, a dispute between an elderly male and female arose. The argument was over a vending spot that was owned by an old man, Mr. Ludvig Resistanse.

Mr. Resistanse had owned this spot for a long time. He was a leather salesman but apparently was not paying his dues to the town management for quite some time now. For more than a week, it was stated by town leaders that he must move out from this market square because of outstanding debts. It so happened that on this busy morning in Lorraine, before Mr. Resistanse arrived at his spot to get ready for business, his sales spot was already invaded and occupied by another vendor.

An old woman of about seventy years of age by the name of Rufeena Dupree had already installed her advertisement of fur sales. Mrs. Dupree had paid the town leaders her dues for her commerce to begin in this particular spot that was owned by Mr. Resistanse.

At the beginning of the day, business was going great for Mrs. Dupree as people filled the streets because of the flourishing of business in Lorraine when Mr. Resistanse showed up for business.

He asked Mrs. Dupree, raising his hands at her, "What in heavens are you doing in my vending spot, old woman? Don't you know I have owned this location for many years? You can't just barge in here as if you own the land. I want you to and leave at once! Go somewhere else and take your rubbish." pick up your rubbish

Mrs. Dupree was attending a shopper and was not paying much attention to Mr. Resistanse. This made him angry. "Did you hear me, witch? I said get out of my spot!" he shouted much louder and started coughing because of his anger.

Shortly after that, Uriel and Urvenus came along, making sure everything was marching on properly. After all, they were the ones who restored this town back to normal. Before they came close to the scene of the argument, Mr. Resistanse had already torn apart a fur table of Mrs. Dupree's belongings and was stamping it on the ground, getting it dirty.

As Mrs. Dupree was about to beat her grouchy opponent with a stick over his head, Urvenus held the weapon and revoked it from Mrs. Dupree. For if she would have hit her rival with that stick, she could have injured or even killed the elderly bundle of hatred.

Mrs. Dupree was a new arrival from another town but had the rights to occupy the same spot of Mr. Resistanse. At the moment, the old lady felt the weapon was taken away from her. She was so upset that she spat on the face of Urvenus for disabling her to retaliate against her opponent, Mr. Resistanse.

Mr. Resistanse shouted at Urvenus, "See what she did to you, ma'am? She is a witch. Why don't you spit on her as well so she learns a lesson."

Urvenus did absolutely nothing in response to this bitter old woman spitting on her, for the dignity of Urvenus was incomparable to this earthling. However, this argument was not over yet, as Mr. Resistanse wasn't about to give up his longtime vending spot, especially to a woman.

In these days, women had very little rights over men, but the old lady paid her dues, and the vending spot was granted to her.

While Urvenus cleaned off the slime on her face, Mr. Resistanse took out a fire lighter and lit a piece of furry material next to him, as he intended on burning down the entire facility. In a split second, Urvenus simply wrapped her hands around the growing flame. Steam came out from in between her knuckles as the fire was put out instantly.

Uriel stood watching at these two fighters patiently, but he had enough of these old geezers. He went up to them and touch both of them right in the center of the facility, and they were suddenly found in the middle of a large open savannah filled with nothing but cows and horses, as they were transferred along with all their facility to a place where no business was possible. They were both abandoned in the middle of nowhere because of their immature behavior.

One minute after, Uriel reappeared in the marketplace with Urvenus. Urvenus didn't know exactly where her brother had taken those two earthlings. But she knew that wherever Uriel had taken them, they would have to end their conflicts.

CHAPTER 13

As the two extraterrestrials drifted away, someone came to them with a telegram from Alsace. The message was from Tandoor, who was not seen by Uriel and Urvenus for some time now and who wrote about a friend they met in the city of Alsace, one called Boris Iluvious. It was understood that Boris was very ill and about to die due to an illness. Amazingly, Uriel and Urvenus did not even have to open the message, for they already knew what was the matter. The news about Boris was known by the one who brought the message. Uriel and Urvenus remembered their buddy very well and made their way to Alsace right away, for everything in Lorraine seemed to be going well. At a distance from all the bustling of the commercial area, these two warriors took off, straight up into the heavens with a powerful force. It appeared that Tandoor was residing in the same city as Boris, because the message was sent by her.

Just a couple of moments after, Uriel and Urvenus made contact to ground level right in front of the home of Boris. Many people were there, visiting the sick man, for Boris was well-known by many people due to his isolated lifestyle from much of his fellow humans. When these two extraterrestrials came near, everyone cleared the way with much caution and a bit of fear.

The wife of Boris, who was once a street woman, had turned her life around and cared for her husband with deep regrets of wasting away years of her life to nothing but distortion and corruption instead of living an honorable life. Delylah welcomed Uriel and Urvenus into the humble home of their sick friend, although she was a little nervous on what these two individuals would do once inside.

A voice for Urvenus, it was Tandoor who was sitting inside in a dark corner of the house.

Urvenus held her friend from the shoulders and said, "It is a pleasure to see you again, my friend. How have you carried along throughout these days?"

Tandoor replied happy but at the same time very much depressed. "I am doing well, my friend, but our new friend, the tender old man Boris, is dying very quickly, and it makes me hurt to see such a good man die."

Uriel stood next to his sister, listening to what was said, but did not understand why everyone was at the home of Boris.

The people who were at the home of Boris were mourning because death was in the air, as it was coming for Boris.

Uriel himself was a little confused at this activity. He looked around with those intimidating deep-black eyes as he tried to understand what so many visitors were doing in one home at the same time. Uriel knew nothing about the emotions that a human would encounter when a loved one would leave the physical world.

Everyone inside the house of Boris stared greatly at the outfit used by these advance individuals from the unknown. Some of them spoke secretly among themselves, being very careful that Uriel or Urvenus would not notice their curiosity.

According to Delylah, Boris wasn't able to walk or make reason of anything or anyone around him because of his closeness to death. The room in which the sick man was situated was now clear for Uriel and Urvenus to enter.

When they entered the room, Boris slowly turned his head to see who it was. Although he could not speak any longer, something strange happened when Uriel and Urvenus entered the room. The ill man had recognized them and spoke with great difficulty, "Even to speak I use great strength. That is why I chose not to. But for creatures like you, I have to say it was the most interesting and exciting moment for me at the lake. Presently, I am drifting farcher away from this world, as my life is coming to an end."

Uriel said to his sick friend, "Your mobile existence comes to an end, an end that is the beginning of a genuine but abstract life source that has given you power throughout your earthly life. Now you are afraid of what lies beyond a heartbeat, for I say that your death is that on the other side of physical life."

Boris listened attentively while he lay on his bed. On certain moments, he smiled slightly, for he was very glad that he had the privilege to be acquainted with what would be known today as extraterrestrials. "Many people around you do not even know how important you are on our earth, but now I have understood your quest vividly. My comrades have never paused to think that perhaps their ruthless action would cause a violent reaction outside our atmosphere," said Boris.

Urvenus said, "Boris, my friend, you have been a special creature on your earth with great accomplishment that shall be of special ranks to you in the future. Be not afraid of your journey that awaits you. Perhaps we could be granted the wish to visit you in your new world, for it is dependent on a power source that our own elders on Sedna could never be able to reach."

Boris was relieved on what was said to him, because he believed these creatures were extremely far more informed than anyone on earth at that time.

Uriel moved backward just a few feet from the bed of Boris, for he wanted to see the health status of his friend. He stared at Boris very profoundly with extreme focus as he penetrated meat and muscles on the body of Boris with what was known as ultra-thermal vision. Uriel found that all body organs were working properly, except for a heart pulp that was beating slow for a regular middle-aged human. Uriel and Urvenus walked out of the room.

Standing nearly at seven feet tall, everyone looked at Uriel thinking that perhaps he was capable of healing Boris and thus saving him from certain death. Suddenly, Delylah rushed to Uriel with cries for desperation, asking for Boris to be healed and his life to be spared.

Urvenus held her and strangely blew ice-cold wind into the face of Delylah. With this being done, the desperate woman was calm and fell asleep almost instantly.

Tandoor, who was still present, asked Uriel if nothing could be done for Boris. Of course, she referred to the abilities that Uriel was capable of doing, for many people spoke about what they had seen on some occasion.

Uriel answered, "I cannot and am not authorized to reverse that which has been ordained by the Almighty. If on our planet, perhaps it would be possible, but as you can see, our species are very distinct and manufactured differently with a different evolution and final stage. Your kind lives another life after this existence. Our kind lives on. We are exterminated but also have the option to be regenerated as well, simply through a modification with special rules to follow."

A short while later, as Uriel and Urvenus stood on the street both facing the home of the sick friend, a loud cry was heard. Boris had died peacefully in his sleep at the age of seventy-eight.

A few other people were weeping along with the widow. The scenery inside the house was very confusing, as everyone was alarmed and some crying even without knowing who Boris was.

Uriel himself was a bit confused as well, for on Sedna this process was very different, although his kind also perished in time. Perhaps it was because they had an option that had been used as normal part of their existence while humans had no idea what happened at the point of death. Or could it be that Uriel and his creation go through the same painful process as we do on earth but simply look at death from another point of view? Having the ability to travel into any dimension they wished, perhaps in the future humans might be able to know this mystery, but first we must make open contact with them on a regular basis. According to Uriel himself, when death would arrive, another unseen life would begin for all humans while not for his kind.

Funeral arrangements were made immediately, for Boris was to be buried the next day. Urvenus and Uriel remained very much out of the way since they had no idea about the process of a human burial. They stood in the middle of the road, just looking on with keenness.

An old man walked by. As he did, he looked up at Uriel and said, "You know, you should have a little more respect for the dead!" Walking away slowly, once more, he said to himself, Scaring everybody in a sad moment like this. Darn devil worshipers!

The two extraterrestrials said absolutely nothing in respect to the words of this old man; moreover, they didn't even bother to make out what the old man said to them, for they were trying to understand what would cause a human to fall under a state of sadness when one of their kind passed on.

Delylah was in tears the entire time due to the lost of her husband. Perhaps what was more painful to her was that she wasted a precious part of her life to a world of impurity, darkness, and immorality.

As night settled in, Urvenus lowered her brow slightly as she disappeared along with Uriel while mourners accompanied the new widow.

As the morning hours arrived, a rough wooden casket was brought to the home of Boris, for the procession was about to begin toward a cemetery nearby. Just when the body of Boris was being taken out of the house, two beams of laser lights made ground contact with a thundering sound right in front of the funeral, blocking the way. Right at this moment, a number of men were loading the coffin unto a carriage that was to be pulled by two horses; unfortunately due to the fright of this sudden apparition by the extraterrestrials, the wooden box holding the dead was heavily dropped to the ground.

The feet of one of the helpers was also smashed like a pancake, and he groaned in pain, all because of two creatures from another planet that didn't quite know about the state of humans when a loved one would die.

Uriel said nothing as he stood in front of everyone, wondering what these locals were up to with an old wooden box holding his friend. Urvenus apologized for their sudden appearance, but that was the only way they would make their arrival at a particular destination. As for Uriel, he did not have any knowledge about respect for the dead on the earth, and for that being so, he said nothing in respect to apologies; instead he stood right in the way of the funeral.

Urvenus was a little more aware about what the humans were doing; she had seen a few of these activities whenever people would die but never understood clearly that it was a sad time for friends and family members. Uriel was removed by his sister from the path of the procession, but they both followed behind from a distance.

They wanted to see where would be the final resting ground for their cherished friend.

On arrival at the graveyard, Uriel began to understand what was happening, although not quite as he thought. Most cadavers were placed inside a tomb, but for Boris, because his wife and sister did not have enough money to build one, he was simply going to be thrown into a deep hole that was dug days ago. He was simply going to be inserted into the ground with tons of dirt dumped over him.

These individuals from space watched closely from outside the group of weeping people on what was being done. I tell you, they were not happy at all. The fingertips on Uriel were crisping with electricity; this normally happened when he would become agitated. Just when the body of Boris was being lowered into the hole, Uriel moved into the group of people and froze the wooden box instantly. Astonishingly, it remained afloat about three feet over the deep and dark hole. Apparently, he thought that it was not proper for a human to be lowered into the ground after death.

Confusion arose at this action. Everyone was afraid and distorted at the two extraterrestrials. On the other hand, some were slightly upset because their ritual was being interrupted repeatedly.

Uriel and Urvenus did know it took so much money to erect a marked grave for a loved one. Some people ran away in fright. Perhaps they thought that being in a graveyard with creatures from outer space would be like asking for trouble.

Tandoor was there, standing next to Delylah, but they were surprised as well as everyone else, although they knew very well that Boris was somewhat cared for and appreciated by the funeral crushers.

Delylah walked up to them cautiously and said, "Mister and missus, on earth, it is a traditional process for a burial in a cemetery like this one. Perhaps it seems wrong and abnormal for you both to see a dead human being lowered into the ground and have dirt scattered over him or her, but it is the way it has been done for many generations! Now tell me, why did you stop the final stage of this funeral?"

Uriel replied, "Your companion in earthly existence was of great importance to us, for his peaceful beginning and end is what we seek; therefore, it is our will to preserve his visible remains above the level of knads-and-flesh-eating creatures!"

Delylah answered, "In your hands, he shall be fine; do as you wish."

With that being said, Uriel navigated his right arm from left to right with a small shining object. A beautiful icy cube was erected out of nothing before their very eyes. This was erected just under a minute, beneath a willow tree. Uriel then went to the wooden casket in which Boris was laid. As he opened the lid, Urvenus joined him on the opposite side of the box and placed both their hands over Boris. Slowly, the body of the old man vanished from inside the casket; it then reappeared seconds after inside the icy cube. It was clearly a transfer from one container into the other, only that it was done without touching the body.

This thing in which the body of Boris now lay was clearly from another world. It was clear as ice from the outside, but after about five minutes, Boris could not be seen anymore, for the walls on this thing became thicker and steamier. The one thing that was difficult to accept was that this icy tomb was completely afloat above ground. Perhaps something like this was used for deceased creatures on the planet where Uriel and Urvenus came from. To recall what Uriel said on one occasion, pertaining to this wonder, he stated that their kind, after terminated, were locked inside transparent shields that were suspended above the ground, and some of which were even brought back to life. As to how this was done, most likely we would never find out.

Delylah was quite happy to see that her husband was going to have a unique grave like no other on the face of the earth. But she still wondered if Boris was to be preserved, then what shall happen after many years?

Uriel knew what Delylah was thinking and responded to her thoughts, "Your husband cannot be regenerated due to very different molecules in his body, and the circumstances of expiration are normal due to human aging. Moreover, I do not have the power neither the authority to do this on your world. I only gave our friend a more comfortable resting domain. His flesh and bones will perish in about one earth year, for he was not preserved to be restored. His tomb as you call it shall also perish, but by then you shall not be on this earth any longer."

Delylah was astonished and a bit confused at the words of Uriel, but she still agreed with no questions asked. Everyone who was there at that moment was completely amazed. A few even fainted.

Not too long after the burial was over, Boris was on his way into perhaps a higher stage of existence. Delylah had to continue with her life on her own until her turn came around.

CHAPTER 14

As Uriel and Urvenus made their way back into the city, an enormous army of local authorities blocked their way. Uriel and Urvenus were being accompanied by Tandoor, for the incident concerning Boris was recently over.

The head officials were guarded by some fifty or sixty high-ranking officers, armed with swords. The army and their greedy general had nothing to do with this, for this confrontation probably had something to do with that poor helpless individual back in Providence.

As Uriel stared at these lawmen, he knew instantly that some of them were the very same ones that wanted to execute an innocent human, for they were trying to prevent blackmail. Since Uriel was not too far away from the execution site, the authorities believed that he and his companion were also involved due to supernatural activities.

A few of the authorities with swords in their hands were in a constant trembling motion due to the fact that they were very informed about unbelievable resistance from these two creatures.

The news were heard all over this French region about these extraterrestrials taking gunshots and having bullets smashed on the tip of their fingers, moreover cannonballs landing almost on top of them, causing absolutely no harm.

Nevertheless, these men had to obey their orders, no matter who it was they're up against.

The high chief of authority spoke in a loud voice, "We were sent to place you both under arrest on direct orders from the emperor himself. If you resist, you will be shot repeatedly!"

Tandoor said angrily, "These beings have done nothing wrong. Instead, they are doing you, all, a favor in restoring order to many towns. Missions that you have strived to accomplish in a lifetime are done with ease by these individuals. I did not state that on many occasions, you have twisted the laws of this country for your own convenience as well."

The high chief in command was not pleased at all with Tandoor, as he seemed about to explode with anger. These lawmen knew that to lose their temper in this situation would compromise their quest. They figured that Uriel and Urvenus already knew the reasons why they wanted to kill that innocent family man since the young son of the ex-captive interacted with them.

Urvenus looked very focused on these authority figures, as if she was ready for showdown once again. Uriel and his companion had much patience with these earthlings, for their mission would be a failure if they were to extinguish a creature from the planet earth. Their intellectual state of living was far more advance than ours. Due to their status in the outer universe, they were chosen to eradicate the residue left behind by the hostile and dark actions of earth creatures, not to mention the effects these were causing on their home front. It was obvious that their mission was far too delicate to be put in jeopardy, for this would be certain if they would reduce themselves to the ignorance and greed of earthlings. The high chief shouted a second time, "Have you not heard me? You must come with us. I care very little about your capacity to retaliate. We shall see if you dare to defy the emperor."

Another official said to the chief in charge, "Please, sir, be not aggressive with these individuals, for I believe that if they were to revolt against us, even with reinforcement, we would not live to see another day."

The high chief paid no attention to his comrade, for his position as a law-enforcement official was at stake. The chief official ordered two of his assistants to place Uriel and Urvenus under arrest, although Urvenus was not touched at all. In those days, women were not to be disrespected by any means, even if the country's law was involved.

Now, to underestimate this being from another world because of a gender status would be a costly error. Urvenus had the strength equivalent to five hundred fully grown men, based on physical power. As for Uriel, his force could level an entire army in less than a couple of minutes; nevertheless, these local authorities were certain that they were beyond the power of Uriel.

The high chief commanded Uriel to move ahead of him. Guarded by four officers, Urvenus right by his side seemed to be in a telepathic state of communication.

Some authority officers walked side by side with the prisoners but still kept their distance; they knew that their captives could be very dangerous. Uriel probably knew where they were being taken, but being who they were, nothing and no one could intimidate them.

Urvenus had her hands on a deadly sword of her own located beneath her long battle coat; it was as if she was simply awaiting for danger threat to uprise.

Uriel looked at her and slightly nodded his head, perhaps telling her the time had not yet come to retaliate.

Some local residents of Alsace came out of their homes and tried to prevent these individuals from being prosecuted, for they knew very well that Uriel and Urvenus came to eradicate darkness from their land. These people came to like the extraterrestrials so much that they were willing to confront their own emperor to save their long-distance visitors. Clearly, these creatures from afar were icons unto the eyes of many humans, funny that the extraterrestrials were not even aware of it, and if they did, perhaps they didn't even care.

a comment on Some officers pointed their pistols at people to show their domination, including a young man of about twenty-five years of age who received a fist on the mouth for making the corruption of law-enforcement and governing officials. Uriel and his sister remained very calm and mellow, as if it was simply a walk in the park. But with all their power and strength, who wouldn't be?

A short while after, the prisoners were brought before a great mansion in the very same city of Providence. This estate was located in a very wealthy neighborhood. About half a dozen guards came to the large gates of this mansion to receive their captured individuals. These high-ranking officials were the emperor's guards, all appearing very serious in character, with elegant uniforms and fancy head dressing. They were trained to show no humor, no fear, and certainly no mercy to no one, and under no circumstances.

In this era of the early eighteen hundreds, the emperor and his men were the most powerful force to reckon with in the European continent, not only in France but also in Germany and Rome.

Napoleon was establishing his own empire as well, which later in time came to be one of the most evil and dominant forces in the history of mankind, only to be later terminated by a new power who made its presence felt through the entire Middle East.

Since these guards were trained to show no fear and no mercy, who they were about to meet would not be a regular criminal from earth but those who had traveled many light-years at the speed of light from a distant galaxy.

When they laid eyes on Uriel and Urvenus, even as they tried to stare fearlessly into the eerie eyes of a beast, it was irresistible for them to show forth some concern on who these beings were. It was obvious for the guards that their captives were like no other, as an eerie feeling came over them. Even with this being so, their pride in who they were was still beyond their intelligence.

One of the guards went up to Uriel and tried to disarm him while another cranked his pistol and pointed it directly to the forehead. These earthlings had now sealed their fate by doing this. Just when this guard was about to remove that extremely powerful weapon extended forward from the shoulder of this alien, his entire face was literally smashed in to the back of the head by a tremendous blow on behalf of this creature.

The guard fell dead unto the ground after crashing into some concrete walls, since his eyes disappeared into the rear of his skull. Two more guards attacked Uriel as they tried to overpower him, but they were both flung some fifty feet away, landing headfirst into the bare concrete floor. Their neck bone was shattered as they died almost instantly.

These well-trained guards were being eliminated in multiple numbers, for their aggression and violent actions were all that was needed for those extraterrestrials to retaliate. This activity was happening even within the emperor's estate, precisely at the gated entrance. This mammoth building was so huge that even gunshots couldn't be heard from one area to another. The guards that Uriel had just eliminated were some of the very best in the emperor's army. Unfortunately, their wisdom was against them on this fatal day. The officials who brought in the captives told the guards not to provoke the extraterrestrials because they would indeed revolt. Going back into the past, Uriel himself stated that the power of their retaliation should not be tested, for catastrophic results would be certain.

These guards had to render respect to these extraterrestrials just the same as they did to the emperor. When they were brought into the presence of the emperor, they were ordered to bow to his majesty, the emperor of France. This emperor was of more than forty years of age but very cunning, greedy, and ruthless as well.

He was in constant contacts with other rulers from neighboring countries, especially Napoleon, emperor of Germany. As he sat on his royal throne, even with all his grandeur and wealth, he was struck at the stunning sight of these new captives. He even stood up from his chair, with his eyes focused on who or what was in his presence. He knew instantly that they were not regular citizens from nearby. To think about this matter, even the emperor and his army were in no standards of comparing might and power with these most wanted individuals.

These creatures were far more advanced with wisdom and technological engineering than any emperor, scientist, or earthly organization could hold, for theirs was heavenly and not man-made.

When this emperor descended from his seat down to where Uriel and Urvenus were standing, even being slightly in wonder on what he should do, he still commanded these two extraterrestrials to kneel before him. His order went up in smoke, for this was not going to happen.

Why? Because these creatures would not and had never taken orders from humans; moreover, they cared very little about who was beyond who on the earth. Their mission must be accomplished no matter who they needed to extinguish. According to Uriel, his galaxy and planet was feeling the effects of unacceptable human behavior.

Urvenus stood with great majesty herself, armed with an arsenal of weapons from out of this world, some of which the emperor could not take his eyes off.

The guards walked cautiously and fearfully toward Uriel. Instead of ordering him to kneel before the emperor, they begged and pleaded with him to do so, for they saw what happened to their friends just outside the mansion. When the guards realized that orders were not being taken by these individuals, they knew something terrible was about to happen.

The emperor spoke, "I have been told that you both are extremely powerful! I don't know who you are as of now, but I will! Our people believe that you both came from another planet; I tell you right now, I do not care where it is you came from!" This emperor was making a mockery of Uriel and Urvenus by laughing cynically at their identity.

The visitors from the unknown remained silent, looking straight into the face of this mighty ruler. The emperor went on to say, "I was also told you perform marvelous actions, most of all clever ones. I tell you now, do not interfere with my orders. Respect my guards and authorities. If you refuse, you shall be dismembered!"

About a dozen armed guards were standing near, with more than two hundred situated just outside the royal courtroom, which indeed looked like a ballroom with costly ornaments. No one had ever answered to the emperor when he or she was spoken to, but in this situation, the prisoners were unique and fearless. The emperor could not stop looking at Urvenus, for her attire and beautiful figure was amazing yet very dangerous and powerful. This man walked in circles around Uriel as well, as if he was trying to understand where such fine wear came from.

Urvenus said with majesty, "If you are such a wise and powerful man, then why do your people suffer from afflictions, poverty, wars, and so much perdition? Perhaps your station is and was a base of forceful entry, for this lofty position suits you not. Or could it be that your followers have lost the essence of dignity and honor?"

The emperor ordered two of his guards to punish Urvenus for what she said. Perhaps Urvenus said the truth about him and that he did not accept, including the fact that it was the first time someone ever returned fire at him.

Two armed men from the group of guards standing by saw what happened to three other guards at the entrance of the mansion due to a confrontation with Uriel. However, this command must be followed, or these guards would also be killed, simply for defying strict orders.

Even as Urvenus appeared as a female, it was a need to understand that her force should not be determined by what she appeared on earth but by who she was on Sedna. She was a little intimidating herself, due to her vesture and strange fingers, not to mention a wide variety of weapons she carried just under her shawl.

A strange metal thing, looking very much like a helmet, was placed on the head of this beautiful vixen named Urvenus. But this was no helmet; it was a head clamp used for torturing. It had two latches attached to it, one on each side. These latches were held open by a spring rod. When this rod was released, the latches would slam shut, smashing the head of the individual with great pressure. As the spring rod was about to be released, she held this entire thick metallic head smasher with both hands and twisted it as if it was made of rubber, crushing it like a cardboard box and throwing it to the ground.

The emperor was astonished and a bit shaken. Perhaps now he believed what his own people were saying about the ones he had in his presence. However, he had to keep his concern hidden, for he thought his position might be at stake.

Even with what he saw, he still gave a command to an entire dozen of his guards to eliminate these individuals. The question was, why was he so persistent that he could destroy these creatures? Uriel said to this emperor for the first time, "It is of no concern to us who you are and the status of your social earthly position. Your might and power can in no wise harm us. Our task on this dust land is to eradicate the backlashes of your ruthless deeds. Whenever earthlings like you are found in the cross battle, there will certainly be human casualties!"

The guards still remained motionless to an attack against these extraterrestrials, at least for the time being, but a horrible fight was clearly on its way.

The emperor was also a clever man. He knew that to be impatient would cost him many guards. He asked Uriel what was his station on earth.

Uriel replied, "A distant modified soldier, in search of dark residue of human deeds, terminating potential dangerous threats to our own existence on our home front galactic circle. As you can see, not even an earthling sitting on a throne disguised with fine wear on the outside but rust on the inside can govern over what he has not created!"

With this being said, the great ruler felt that his high position was insulted by the extraterrestrials. This emperor had more than just regular fighting guards in his arsenal. He was in command of a giant wizard. He used this monster as his ultimate fighting machine. This wizard was a master of black magic or, in other words, works of the devil, which made it invincible. This thing was just under nine feet tall, weighing something like six hundred pounds. This was more of a monster than a man. Similar to Von Seth's existence, people also said that an enormous beast who ate humans resided in the estate of the emperor. Legend had it that this creature was a hardworking man just as all the others, of a normal stature as well. In time, he made a pact with a morbid angel from the dark side to regain his long-lost love who paid him no attention because of difference in social level. His end of the deal was unaccomplished, and for that he was cursed by the devil himself. He lost his sanity and grew to extreme levels over a short period. The emperor captured him, fed him, and later used him as a killing machine against any force that would defy him.

It was not known if Von Seth was the source of this creature's demise. When this thing would walk, it would even crack the ground beneath its feet. Being filled with hair throughout its body, and with a bad teeth, it was indeed a frightening sight. Its force was evil and very potent to anyone.

As the emperor stood facing Uriel and Urvenus, he said in an angry voice, "Let's see if you can withstand the wrath of Borg!" He called out this beast from its underground domain. The thundering sound could be heard as it made its way up the stairway to the surface.

When this thing came within visible range of the extraterrestrials, they locked sight on one another. Uriel was a large individual but was still about twelve inches below the stature of this monster and well below five hundred pounds.

As Urvenus made a stand against this creature, it made a growling sound of many vocals while stomping its feet on the floor, vibrating the walls of the mansion.

Urvenus moved back just a bit, since it was probably their most difficult challenge on the earth since Von Seth. The guards left at that moment, for they knew that a gruesome fight was to begin, leaving just the emperor, his beast, and the extraterrestrials to square off.

The emperor commanded this animal to destroy the two extraterrestrials. This thing called Uriel and Urvenus by hand motion from about ten feet away, for it couldn't speak.

Uriel faced this creature with absolutely no fear, for he never backed down from anything. His eyes turned totally black with his arms extended downward as electricity crisped on his fingertips. Urvenus stood right next to him but slightly intimidated.

Uriel gave three large steps forward to confront this beast, showing his will to do battle. The emperor moved away from among them to a safe distance. The beast named Borg looked at the emperor as if wondering why his opponents look different from all the ones he had murdered.

The emperor was fascinated to see this fight, for what he wanted was to have Uriel and his company removed from his way.

The huge wizard began to move toward Uriel, ferociously clobbering him across the spine with a long iron rod soaked into something called fairy dust that was mixed with some kind of solution so that it would hold on to iron material.

Uriel was down on the floor due to the powerful blow and the potency of this strange dust. Shockingly, he rose instantly as if he was lifted by an unseen force back to his feet.

The giant wizard attacked once again as he tried to smash Uriel by throwing him into the walls by the movement of his arm. It had no effect on Uriel, but it had on Urvenus. She was flung straight up through a concrete ceiling, creating a hole on the lower roof of this mansion before falling back to the ground.

Uriel saw this and fired a beam of laser from his state-of-the-art catastrophic weapon, causing a huge explosion on impact with this creature called Borg.

The entire mansion collapsed to the ground due to the shock wave blast, killing everyone inside, including the emperor. Amazingly, this wizard was still alive but was missing most of his body parts, as it lay very wounded on the ground, yet insisting to continue doing battle against Uriel and his assistant. His entire head was crushed into the floor when Uriel stepped on it with his large boot. Its long feet vibrated a little as its brain burst out on to the floor. One more victory for these great warriors.

As they walked out of the wreckage, some people came near the place where the mansion once stood to see what had happened, for even homes nearby suffered moderate damage due to the destruction caused by this beast from outer space.

Nothing but piles of rubble and mutilated bodies were recovered by other government organizations. The news about the terrible death of this wicked emperor and some members of his own army had spread rapidly into other countries, including information about who caused such tremendous devastation. Uriel and Urvenus didn't respond to any human questioning, for no one dared to ask them. Everyone was warned in the past to stay clear from in between their battles with dark entities as well as testing their strength.

CHAPTER 15

These two creatures were undefeatable on the earth. They blasted away into the heavens, leaving a long line of dust or perhaps smoke behind. They had returned to meet with Tandoor in Alsace.

During the past few days, the general was unheard of, and so was his army. Perhaps they knew better now about getting in the way of the visitors from the unknown. After all, it was for their own safety and healthy living.

Tandoor greeted her friends once again. They were happy to see Uriel and Urvenus, for the residents of this fortified city of Alsace were rattled over the last few days due to some frightening demon like creatures roaming certain parts of the town. Tandoor stated that all of them had half their faces sort of missing and with very long fingers.

Uriel knew it was his father's army of Avisteroids that were rescued from the Wastelands.

During this time, Lorraine had become enriched with fortified fields of crops. The main city was tidy and sanitary. Most inhabitants were now hardworking people and becoming very intelligent, not to mention that even exportation was getting underway directly out of Lorraine to other countries.

Uriel and Urvenus were victorious, for they had succeeded in restoring the proper functions of this once-ravaged town and its residents.

Providence was also flourishing with peace and harmony among the people who lived there now that there was no ruthless emperor.

Other places where Uriel had done his wonders also included Ireland and London, England, also known as Great Britain. It was said by many English men that while Uriel was in London, he had completely wiped out a number of vampire clans.

Many people did not believe in the existence of these bloodsucking creatures until Uriel took them out in great numbers, leaving them roasted inside and out, lying dead on city streets. Police officers and detectives were investigating the horrific murders before Uriel made his presence known. Each night, a high number of local English people would die within the city limits with puncture wounds around the upper spinal area. The ones responsible for these gruesome crimes were still at large due to speed, intelligence, and great strength, at least it was so until Uriel entered the city limits. Urvenus was not with him at the time, for these unfamiliar activities in London took place some time after he wandered away from his father and his henchmen from hell. The two icons met at the site of a lighthouse where a small encounter took place between once Indrid Cole and some creatures called keepers of the bay.

It was unknown if Uriel and Urvenus were actually born from Celine, much more if something of this nature took place on the earth. Uriel had said that a birth took place but very different from our own; he never explained the details of what he meant, although he made it to be understood that they were more of a spiritual existence rather than that of flesh and bones but were still a creation from the all-powerful.

By now, great numbers of territorial citizens were beginning to understand the destructive effects of environmental personal destruction. However, France and its neighboring countries were surely not alone in the battle against negative and dark forces.

The entire planet of earth contained many nations and continents, and for unknown reasons, France was a primary target on the radars of those from the outer universe.

Have in mind that evil existed all around the world, but Uriel directly and his assistants were sent to the French territory. Perhaps was to be left for someone who would be sent the rest of the planet on direct command form the Creator in years to come.

It could have been that Martians patrolling the galactic circle of the Trifid Nebula detected extreme chaos and genocide originating directly from the European territory. This statement was more of a fact-based information because in the past decades before the existence of Leena, later known as Celine, and her offsprings were recognized on the earth, it was heard from a number of farmworkers and hunters in the forest that an enormous diamond-shaped object with thousands of flickering lights or lasers was seen from a distance, making land fall several miles into the forest. A short moment after, it rose to treetop level for a few minutes and then shot straight up into the heavens before a second breath could be taken.

Uriel and Urvenus remained in the hometown of the late Boris.

Tandoor kept staring at her secret love but never insisted to find a way for him to look at her with the eyes of a typical earth man. She had to understand that her dreams about becoming the bride of Uriel was just not possible, even if Uriel himself wanted it to be so.

Throughout all the past years, Uriel had never seen or met his father as a well-developed Martian. Urvenus did not even know about the existence of a father, much more being abandoned centuries ago on the earth by his own kind. This was not to continue for long, as a confrontation between Blane Shacks and his own son perhaps was not too far away, thus allowing young Urvenus to know the truth.

The Avisteroids were not many, but their power was equal as if they were a thousand. It was twenty, possibly thirty, that were rescued from the Wastelands. A fraction of their faces were scarred due to gruesome battles in the abyss, or hell if you will. These were like humans, except for their immense strength and disfigured faces.

Uriel and Urvenus traveled to the cemetery where their friend Boris was laid to rest inside his unique tomb from outside this world, apparently there to do something not known to that strange icy container. It would hold his remains for a long time until his body vanished through a sanitary process.

A few other locals were visiting their loved ones who had perished.

Uriel stared at them, wondering why they were paying tribute to a place where nothing but bones resided.

Urvenus looked at him and said, "I see you in great wonder, my brother! This is a place for those earthlings who are removed from this plane of flesh and bones. Unto us, it surfaces as an error, but for these earthly creatures, it is a mere tradition upheld by their humanity for thousands of years. Our zenith grounds are very different from theirs due to differences in specie and technology."

Uriel moved his head to the right slightly as he pointed his right hand toward the rest of the graves, as if feeling for something in the air above them. He walked toward the people who were visiting, and he was shown much gratitude, although some of these folks were still a bit afraid and slightly uncomfortable because of their presence, especially being in a burial ground. Uriel asked in a gentle but heavy tone of voice, "Do you, earth creatures, encounter alleviation from your sorrows and grief by rendering devotion to a concrete object that no longer holds them who have perished?"

A woman who had visited her father's tomb for many years replied, "Mister, it is a way to show that they are still remembered and that they remain in our hearts forever!"

Uriel answered, "I will say to you, all, that a resting ground holds only the corpse of your diamonds, but the remembrance of its brilliance lives within you, all. After your diamonds have been lost to extinction, the envision of its beauty remains in that memory of yours. This power is adapted to humanity's most efficient abstract reality. This blessing for you, earthlings, will one day be understood to a certain reach but never to its core, for it comes from a source I shall not mention!"

A few people standing next to him understood just a small portion of what he said, for these folks were still too wayward to captivate this explanation.

Urvenus listened attentively, as well as Tandoor who was also with them. Tandoor understood with clarity what was said, for she could be seen eager to hear more of the human connection to this awesome invisible source.

A few minutes later, a strange being entered the graveyard, accompanied by a large group of assassins all dressed in black robes with blue outlines around the collar. It surely was Blane Shacks with his evil Avisteroids. They made a confrontation to Uriel and Urvenus by upholding a scepter above their heads.

Blane knew Uriel was his descendant but did not seem to care. The people who were there visiting ran away immediately, for they knew another war was to take place shortly.

Uriel laid out his hand to Urvenus and said, "I have seen all your engagements on this earth from within the reservoir of a foreseen future since you were a youngster. I saw your powers gaining strength as time extended, leading to what you are now. Even if the outcome to this war never ends, I say to you your support is embraced."

Urvenus had an idea that it might be her father who just entered the graveyard accompanied by evil creatures, but she also knew he was evil because of his warlords.

Meanwhile, Uriel stared right into his father's eyes with neutral emotion. After all, these creatures were not created as humans with fluctuating emotions but rather that of fearless bounty hunters in search of wars against evil.

This time it was slightly different, as the primary target was that of his own. Uriel, a noble warrior sent to earth perhaps in his mother's womb, having been raised as a young boy in the middle of a skeletal world, was now face-to-face with his estranged father.

Blane Shacks was sent to earth and left for dead a great number of centuries ago because of failing to follow orders from his great elders on Sedna. Those from the underworld standing next to him were eager to terminate Uriel, but the word to proceed was not yet given.

Uriel said to his father, "Have you come to take me into your circle of fire? Or have you come to extinguish your harvest? Why have you forsaken us, Father? You were a leader of great legions guarding and protecting our universe. As a punishment for your broken loyalty, you must now remain on this land of greed and envy."

Blane didn't seem to care much about what Uriel had to say. Although he appeared as a very serious, majestic king, a tear streamed down from his eyes when he laid eyes on Urvenus. Blane could feel the suffering of envy, jealousy, hatred, and the need for dominion, just as all humans. This poisoned him even longer, as his demons became stronger.

Without warning, all warlords standing next to Blane attacked Uriel and Urvenus with flame shooting out of their bare hands. Urvenus blew the fire out with her ice-cold breath before it made contact with them.

Uriel launched his deadly spears from beneath his battle gear. Amazingly, these things didn't need power from any motorized mechanism, for all he did was open his long robe, and these iron rods would appear firing from an area beneath his huge arms.

More than half a dozen spears were inserted into more than six Avisteroids right on their foreheads at very great speed. They were even pushed back to the ground because of such force. Note that these spears were launched all at once, obviously reloading the same amount that was used invisibly. Clearly, these creatures were extremely powerful.

Six Avisteroids were erased from the face of the earth, with more than a dozen remaining. Nevertheless, those that remained were slightly hesitant about proceeding.

Blane Shacks was just standing there, doing absolutely nothing while his henchmen tried eliminating his son and daughter.

Urvenus made her own attack by rising into the air with two short fighting swords in her hands slicing the heads of two more Wastelanders. They were unable to protect themselves because Urvenus moved as lightning.

The casualties were now eight, with some thirteen of them or more remaining. These creatures were given orders telepathically by Blane, since they make their actions without speaking. Blane simply stood in between the battle. Untouched by any dangerous object, it was almost as if he was protected.

During a struggle, Urvenus was blasted away about twenty feet, landing on top of a grave. Apparently, she was hit on the head by one of the Avisteroids.

Uriel returned one of his own blows, but his was much more severe and deadly, for when he did, the head of his enemy was completely torn off his body. Shockingly, their blood appeared very dark blue in color, rather than red as our own. The remaining Avisteroids were instantly blasted into nonexistence by Uriel's explosive weapon, as it moved in all directions his head would turn. The explosion was so strong that even sepulchers were shifted from their original position.

Blane was now alone and possibly at war with his own offsprings.

Strangely, Uriel did not make an attack against his father. Instead, he held Urvenus by the hand and shimmered out of this graveyard that had become a battleground.

Uriel later awaited for Blane Shacks just outside the city limits of Alsace. Just at this time, the general and his battalion arrived at the same location where the extraterrestrials stood. The army became aware that something had happened due to the thundering sounds that rippled through the air for many miles.

Blane, dressed as a royal king among his defeated followers, wore a bright blue with red robe, because to him, bright colors showed domination. All his Avisteroids were wiped out at the hands of Uriel and Urvenus. Blane faced his offsprings once again on the outskirts of Alsace, just as Uriel intended.

Tandoor was at this scene as well, scared to the bone, for she anticipated a horrific fight. The one thing she didn't know was that Uriel and Urvenus were face-to-face with their own father.

A great number of audience flocked to the wide-open savannah not too far away from the cemetery where the war began. Throughout this time, Blane did not move a single part of his body to extinguish his descendants. Possibly somewhere in his being, he knew he couldn't destroy those who had worked so hard at their mission.

The army closed in to investigate what was the matter between these two parties, for the general already knew that when these creatures do battle, many properties would be reduced to rubbles, including their being a potential danger to human lives as well. More than two hundred horsemen armed with pistols and swords sat on their horses behind the general, who was now accompanied by a captain.

No one knew where the general had been since the strange incident with Celine and the prison of lasers. One thing was for sure, the general showed great respect to Uriel and his company.

Uriel and his estranged father locked eyes on each other, with both having the same strange, intimidating, and eerie darkness covering the entire iris. No one knew who was the individual standing before Uriel and Urvenus, but one thing was certain, they were staring at each other with great focus. Needless to say that in those black eyes of Uriel, an unexplained activity was taking place. It was as if he was looking through time in space, for vivid images of planets, galaxies, asteroids, circles of dust and particles could be seen moving through space within the very eyes of Uriel.

Blane was sort of enchanted at this unbelievable activity happening inside the eyes of his son.

The general noticed that Uriel and Blane were up to something unknown, but he saluted Uriel anyway with a hand across the forehead. He then turned to Blane and said, "I don't know who you are yet, but I have an impression that your presence here is of no good. I was informed that you enjoy looking at conflicts on our land. I shall tell you that is happening no more. As long as I live, France will be a better place as in response to wars and corruption. Our own chief and commander will do all he can to execute a new beginning!"

Urvenus was slightly confused at what was happening between Uriel and Blane, for none of them paid attention to what the general said. She did not know what really to expect. Although the Avisteroids tried to eliminate them, up to this moment, their father was sort of undecided.

Suddenly, Uriel spoke to the general, "It is an honor to see you a change man, Mr. General. I can see you leading your men into spiritual victory in the near future. This creature that stands here before you is of my kind. A close connection binds us together; nevertheless, the gates of his world has been shut for him because of betrayal!"

The general still didn't know that Blane Shacks was the father of Uriel (in their own way that is) but noticed that their eyes were identical, just as much as their stature.

Urvenus stared at her father as she made her way toward him. Right when she stood just a few feet away, she extended her hands as if to greet him, but he backed away from her.

Perhaps Blane knew he failed at something that his offsprings had accomplished, and for this he most likely thought of himself as a failure. Blane was already consumed by earthly matters, for he seemed powerful simply because of his unique attire. His extraterrestrial power had diminished dramatically over the centuries.

Urvenus showed very little emotion when her father whom she had never met before turned away from her. Uriel told her the reason why Blane did this. She understood perfectly. She questioned him if their father's rights and honor could be returned to him.

Uriel responded, "You know as well as I do that our elders are the only ones who have the authority to do so. It could take place only if our Blane submits himself to a brain drainage of all his evil and then modified with what he once possessed. We shall see about this!"

Have in mind that the term brain drainage didn't necessarily mean a brain as our own. To them, it was a metaphor, since their existence was very different from that of a human. It was never explained in the past or in the present what really took place when these creatures were in this process, but the fact of this phenomena was that it changed something within the individual. It didn't have anything to do with a physical brain such as that from a human but more of an invisible modification or, rather said, a spiritual transformation.

It was now just over a year since Uriel and Urvenus were reunited and almost a decade since Uriel began his mission in London. Many other wars he had fought around the continent but were simply not recollected.

It was a tense moment for earthlings looking at an evil creature standing in one place without any movements, for they thought that it could come into motion at any time and kill many of them present.

The general asked Uriel what was the matter with Blane, why didn't he move, speak, or even twinkle the eyes.

Uriel answered, "I cannot reveal to you this reason, but I say to you, he is under control by his own power. He is not a threat!"

CHAPTER 16

This was a bright and sunny day, a bit windy as well. Many people were complaining of headache and a strong burning feeling throughout their body. These local residents were saying that this bad feeling had been going on for a very long time. They said that at times, it would go away but would then return days later.

This burning sensation had spread over Lorraine, Providence, and Alsace as well. No one mentioned anything in the past since they believed it was just a regular incommodity caused by changes in the weather.

Suddenly, the general's horsemen were thrown off their horses for no reason. It was as if these animals became very irritated or frightened at something that could not be seen. Seconds after, a very low air pressure was felt descending from above as the ears of people present began bleeding.

Blane lifted his head slightly toward the heavens as he began chanting words loudly in an unknown language. The sunlight became sort of opaque from one horizon to the other with absolutely no clouds in the sky.

Great fear had now set in for many people throughout many cities, towns, and villages, for the atmosphere was very uncomfortable. The winds picked up velocity to about forty or fifty miles per hour, bending trees and lifting dust into the air.

The general himself was scared to death, as he and the captain were struggling against the wind. Numerous livestock such as to the other, as ift goats, cattle, and chickens were running from one end of the open grasslands if they were possessed by some malevolent force. Blane kept chanting loudly in an unknown language while he gazed into the wide-open skies.

Urvenus and Uriel remained motionless, without any kind of concerns on what was happening. Mostly likely, they knew what it was, but surely it wasn't Blane causing this immense phenomena, for he too seemed to know what it was. Apparently, he seemed to be submitting to this activity.

Many people in other locations were also stating that strange and unknown activities were also happening in their towns and cities.

Delylah, who was near Tandoor, held her tightly, as she thought it was the end of the world. Tandoor said to her not to be afraid because Uriel and Urvenus were not concerned at all and that definitely it had something to do with them.

Slowly, an enormous diamond-shaped object shimmered into visibility overhead, just above the tallest trees. This thing was constructed from materials and components that were a mystery to all mankind. This object appeared like a huge city suspended into the air at night, with thousands of flashing lamps operating in a certain flowing pattern. Even as it was still broad daylight, its brilliance even shone brighter than the rays of the sun on the ground. It covered the sun for great distances, even into Lorraine and Providence, which were a few hundred miles apart. This unknown flying vessel was causing the pressure in the air to fall to very dangerous levels, as it created very fierce winds and low visibility across the land. To these people, it was an incredible sight, as well as it would be for us perhaps even up to this day, but in those days, automobiles weren't even around yet, let alone flying objects. Some of the general's troops fired shots at this thing, but when they did, the bullets fell right in front of their gun barrel. Their weapons had no power in them to fire.

Many local residents fainted due to such awesome sight and perhaps even because of the very low pressure in the air, which caused breathing to become shallow. A middle-aged man ran and threw himself in a nearby pond since he thought that God had sent a wraith to punish them for their sins. Leaders in Lorraine were sending telegrams that they too were able to see this diamond-shaped object from another side of the world and that some of their animals were running into the woods.

Blane Shacks seemed as if he was trying to get away from under this thing, although his efforts to escape did not appear to be because of fear but rather for freedom.

At certain moments, he would move like light from one side to another, but wherever he went, a variety of lasers would be shot from this vessel, blocking all his turns. Astonishingly, this mammoth flying vessel was very silent; the only thing that could be heard was a faint humming sound and trees cracking far and near. Some people were even yelling for Uriel and Urvenus to do something, without thinking that perhaps it was their transportation hovering above them.

Damage to vegetation was significant, as well as to some humans, for they had bloody ears and were being thrown around just a bit as well. The general sent a few of his men for reinforcement with cannons, but Uriel instructed him to do otherwise.

Blane was engraved within hundreds of powerful thick and deadly beams of lights, disabling him almost completely. He was just standing in one place as if something else took control of him.

Uriel then called for everyone to listen, for he had information to pass on.

More than a thousand people were at the scene, including the general and his men. Everyone then became aware that they were somewhat safe, so they stood up to their feet with much difficulty, for the winds were still howling, but decreasing slightly.

Uriel opened an unknown object looking like a green-colored screen with strange and odd numbers similar to the roman numerals. As he touched a few keys on the padded screen, the flying object above rose higher into the air. He did this so people would be a little more comfortable. Uriel then spoke, "Earth people, be not afraid, for what you see above you is of no threat! The moment for our departure has come! Our mission has been accomplished. But before we are gone, I must speak to the government officials in whose land I have roamed. This is a request that must not be denied! I will come to you in three earth days! Lorraine is where I shall be."

With this being said, Blane was slowly absorbed by those beams of lasers surrounding him. He was seen no more after a few seconds. It was unknown if he was pulled into this enormous vessel or if he was simply vanquished.

Uriel and Urvenus by his side saluted everyone by placing their hands together as in prayer and lowering their brow slightly. Instantly, they were zapped straight up into this giant object, quickly disappearing from human vision.

Now it was evident where Uriel and Urvenus spent their time when they would vanish for days and sometimes even weeks. Most likely, this very large vessel was residing above the land for a long time, probably for years. It was simply in a stealth mode. This was why at times Uriel would tilt his head up to the heavens as if awaiting for instructions or new objectives.

Tandoor was a bit sad because she knew that Uriel would soon be gone, and there was nothing she could do to prevent this. It was needless to inform that Tandoor was a lonely person on the earth; she had absolutely no one in her life. Her mother and father had passed away years ago, and she was an only child, with no relatives alive.

The general stated that he must give the information to the high chief commander at once, in respect to what the extraterrestrials requested. It would be a certainty that the governments of Ireland, Germany, and perhaps even London would pay interest to this invitation. Sometime later, the word about extraterrestrial residents in France reached the farther western countries.

During this time, western countries were battling a war of their own to establish themselves as democracy and fighting for their freedom from ruthless oppression. The third day was now at hand, and perhaps it was the last day we would see Uriel and Urvenus on the earth.

Just under two thousand people stood in an open area within the limits of Lorraine, eagerly staring toward the heavens, waiting for the beautiful flying vessel to appear.

Their waiting was over, for Uriel and surely his company made their presence felt when their traveling means came into visibility. One more time, the sun became partially covered by this thing hovering above the trees. This time, it situated itself a little higher than previously.

Everyone was astonished, for they had no idea that something so large was capable of sustaining itself in midair without falling to the ground. In a quick glance, not two but three large beams of light hit the ground in front of everyone. This time, it wasn't laser lights. It was more of a bright glowing blue tube, or tunnel if you will. Out of these lighted tubes came Uriel, Urvenus, and none other than Celine.

They were all dressed in black robes with red capes-very elegant and beautiful clothing these beings were able to obtain. And there was a scepter in the hand of Uriel.

Uriel said to everyone present, "Our time has elapsed on your world. Objectives that were given to us have now been acquired. I shall trust in your knowledge in how to operate your world properly without hostility to any of your own kind!

"Believe me when I say to you that actions of the human race have a residue. So many dark activities committed through centuries had engraved in the atmosphere of your planet and far beyond a fierce friction that could not be ignored, brought on yourselves. one that you

"We have terminated the evil in many individuals, primarily those of a supernatural level. I also shall say to the commanding chief of the French region that a new emperor is needed, one with dignity and honor, for with dignity and honor in the human mind, great things can be at easy reach!"

Urvenus did not say a word. She simply stood slightly behind Uriel, just as a soldier guarding his superior.

Uriel also said, "A creature that was sent to your earth long ago had failed to do what was ordained to him; for that, he was stripped of all his rights and was then abandoned on this planet for a very long time. He has now come home to his own. In due to our victory, this was granted. Presently, he is undergoing a process you would not understand!"

Tandoor felt sort of left behind since she was shown much care and importance on behalf of her two extraterrestrial friends.

Celine stood very silent and motionless, listening to what her son was saying, very eerie looking as always but very peaceful as well.

They all saluted the people present one last time by lowering their brow slightly.

Uriel said a few last words, "Have in mind, people of earth, that victory in your existence is not accomplished by domination and a mere lofty position but by a comprehension of what lies beyond what can be seen, for many things of great magnitude is hidden all around you and within you. Seek for it not with hatred and dissident but with compassion and faith! May peace be in your world, earthlings." These were the very words of Uriel, a mighty warrior, in close relation to someone or something who knew it all.

Celine moved forward just a bit and awarded the chief commander of France a shining round object with a flashing row of beautiful lights all around the object, arranged in a unique pattern. Whatever this was for, it would take much intelligence to learn how to operate it, although it might be a source of contact after they were gone.

Uriel and his companions were pulled into the floating vessel by a soft-glowing magnetic tube. In just a couple of seconds, they were completely inside their transportation.

Tandoor was in tears and very devastated due to her only true friends leaving her alone to continue her life on the earth.

Everyone standing at the scene had their eyes wide open as they could not take their eyes off this flying vessel.

Just before the diamond-shaped object took off, Tandoor found herself being sucked up into the space vessel by the very same laser tubes that beamed up the extraterrestrials. Strangely, it was almost obvious that Tandoor was off to a faraway place where humans had only dreamt of visiting.

In the split of a second, the beautiful diamond-shaped flying object disappeared into the heavens with speed that the human eyes could not follow.

No one knew what would be the outcome of Tandoor, but one thing was for sure, she was with someone that she admired so much, and most likely, she would be returned to earth in time to come.

At that very moment, the burning feeling and head pain that many people complained about had disappeared.

Perhaps in the future, we shall meet those who reside outside our galaxy. Let's just hope they will be Uriel and Urvenus.

THE END

EPILOGUE

Ever thought of what lies beyond the Milky Way galaxy?

Ponder on this statement for a moment. To think that our Maker had created this universe simply for just one of his diverse creations and only inhabiting a speckle of space would be like creating the earth for just one human.

Be aware that it has no beginning or end; this has been the greatest wonder for some if not all the world's scientists and explorers. One burning sun sheds light on everything that has life and exists, for without it, we would all perish.

It might be just a matter of time before we face those who share this universe with us. We might just be dedicating too little attention to that which can't be seen.

There is a great difference between something impossible and something that has not happened.